The
SECRET
LIVES
OF EMMA
BEGINNINGS

NATASHA WALKER

The SECRET LIVES OF EMMA

BEGINNINGS

An Arrow book
Published by Random House Australia Pty Ltd
Level 3, 100 Pacific Highway, North Sydney NSW 2060
www.randomhouse.com.au

First published by Arrow in 2012

Addresses for companies within the Random House Group can be
found at www.randomhouse.com.au/offices

Cataloguing-in-Publication Entry details available at the National
Library of Australia.

Cover image courtesy Sebastian Kriete/ImageBrief
Cover design by Christabella Designs
Internal design and typesetting by Post Pre-Press Group
Printed in Australia by Griffin Press, an accredited ISO AS/NZS
14001:2004 Environmental Management System printer

Random House Australia uses papers that are natural, renewable and
recyclable products and made from wood grown in sustainable forests.
The logging and manufacturing processes are expected to conform to
the environmental regulations of the country of origin.

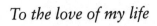

To the love of my life

ONE

Emma Benson had an essay to write. A small book of literary criticism lay unopened on the kitchen table along with a cold cup of coffee and Emma's laptop, which hummed softly as the screen saver displayed the photos from her picture file. A photo from her wedding faded away gradually to be replaced by a blurred shot of a sunset taken with her phone, which in turn was replaced by one of her husband, David, while on honeymoon, standing on the balcony of their hotel room. Suddenly the laptop timed out and shut itself down. The sun-filled room fell silent.

She lay on her beach towel on the grass in the backyard.

An hour earlier an Emma full of good intentions had seated herself at the kitchen table with her notes opened on her laptop. She had read the required texts. She had switched off her phone and had made herself a coffee which steamed within reach. But then she had checked her messages, had read the front page of three newspapers, had opened and scanned through an erotic story she was writing for David, had searched for and found photos she had taken of him which were not in her regular picture folder, but were buried in a locked file. There was a subfolder to this file, with other photos in it, photos of them both and she opened these too.

While flicking through, her mind had drifted a long way from the topic of her essay. There were other buried files, she remembered. Files her husband had never seen. Photos and videos. Memories best hidden from his eyes. She drifted further and further from the task at hand. She grew steadily more agitated and could not sit still. She had to close the files and step away from the computer.

Emma's priorities had changed then. Her labours were postponed indefinitely. The essay no longer seemed as interesting, or important, or as pressing as it once had.

She changed into her bikini, covered herself in suncream, spread out her towel on the grass and, as she had done many times before, lay on her front and beckoned the sun down upon her.

An hour later, Emma still lay on her beach towel on the grass in the backyard. Her face was pressed against the soft towelling and her eyes were closed. The leaves of the huge eucalypt which shaded the back portion of her garden were disturbed by a slight but persistent breeze and someone's wind chimes were jingling nearby. The bikini-clad truant lay in the direct sunlight by the fence out of the draught. A crow launched itself from the eucalypt and cried out far above her as it beat its wings and took flight, crying again and again. The sound, becoming more and more distant, petered out and was exchanged for the rhythmic pock-pock of her neighbour's tennis ball, now hitting the racquet and now the wall. Occasionally the direction of the breeze would change, bringing muted noises of the workmen renovating a house a block away.

All of these sounds played upon her mind,

bearing her in and then out of her daydreams like the tide upon the shore. These daydreams were sweet to her. Quite naturally, her mind had wandered back to the images she had seen. Quite naturally, too, her mind had moved beyond this paucity of remembrance ensnared in hastily taken photos, or in minutes of shaky, poorly lit home video. A deeper reservoir of memories revealed itself to her. Some were reminiscences, some were fictions but most were a seamless mingling of the two. In their coming and going they were altered, emphasis was shifted, episodes were repeated, corrected, bettered, beguiling her senses with newly formed sights and sounds and sensations. Her whole body was responding to the play of her mind. The flesh was deceived.

Having found a suitable theme for idle contemplation, and having moved her hand so that she might touch herself without fear of exposure, Emma drifted off into that place between wakefulness and sleep, which is, when properly directed, a delicious state of near permanent arousal.

Jason dropped over the shared pine paling fence, landed on the soft grass and steadied himself.

4

He noticed that Emma was lying in a bikini on a towel by the table and chairs not two metres away. A closed book and a bottle of 30+ lay beside her.

'Sorry, Mrs Benson, I didn't know you were home,' he said.

Emma was jolted out of her daydreams.

'Shit! Jason. You frightened me,' she said, lifting her head up from the towel to make eye contact and moving her hand from under her. The sun was bright. She lay her head back down and watched his ankles through her eyelashes.

'I didn't know you were here. I lost my ball,' he said, and cast a cursory glance around the garden in search of it. He glimpsed the bare legs, the soft white feet, the small but curvaceous backside barely covered by a white bikini bottom and the long smooth back, but hardly considered them. Pressing and immediate thoughts about the development of his serve and the possibility of switching from cricket to tennis next year hampered his appreciation of these sights. Jason's brain was slow to shift between scenes. Finally, his gaze returned to Emma. And he recognised that she had a beautiful body.

'You could use the gate. That fence is shaky enough as it is without your muscled frame swinging over it,' she mumbled as she closed her eyes.

'Sorry.' He remained still. She could sense him looking at her. She thought about his face as it might look if he was to see her naked. She wondered if Jason had thought about her that way. She waited a time before she felt the silence had lasted long enough for him to have had his fill of her body.

'What are you waiting for? I'm not going to help you. Besides I want to lie here and watch you,' she said, laughing and lifting her shoulders and head to look at him properly. She rested on her elbows with her hands out before her like the sphinx. Her breasts hung in her bikini. Jason did not avert his eyes as an older man might. Emma noticed this and found the youthful naivety of his stare exciting. Her mood shifted from her sleepy indefinite arousal to something more pressing.

'How old are you? I forget,' she asked.

'Eighteen.'

'Did you become an adult without telling me?'

'You were at the party!' he said smiling. He stood on the grass in bare feet, naked but for a small pair of board shorts. Emma watched him; he was growing more and more self-conscious.

She knew she was messing with him. She liked the way his body was developing. He was a very attractive boy who would probably fill out too much as he grew older but now he was lean and toned. She habitually teased him about his looks but it wasn't all play, she genuinely admired his adolescent beauty.

'Have you come over for me or the ball?'

'I didn't know you were home.'

'I'm always home, Jason,' she said, smiling brightly.

'Did you see where the ball went?'

'Nope,' she said and looked around. Emma's garden was large and mostly lawn with garden beds along the edges. She and David were planning to get a landscape architect in; they had been planning to for ages. She looked over into the worst part of the garden under the shade of the eucalypt and saw the ball under a fern. She had no intention of helping him out. He had leapt into her languorous afternoon and in doing so had interrupted an intimate and pleasurable run of imaginary sexual encounters.

Till this moment Jason had only ever drawn a casual appraisal from Emma. He had always remained within his yard, so to speak. He was always the son of Simon and Anne, or the boy next door. But by chance, Jason had grown up and landed squarely in Emma's fantasies. She saw him afresh.

Jason walked around the lawn looking into the mess of a garden. He glanced at Emma over his shoulder and saw her watching him. She blew him a kiss.

'Found it!' he said. She watched him crawl under the fern and pick it up. His body was deeply tanned and as he leant over and stretched out his arm to take hold of the ball his young butt looked good enough, Emma surmised, to eat. She took a mental snapshot.

Jason padded across the grass towards her.

'Don't tell Mum and Dad you saw me,' he said.

'My lips are sealed,' said Emma, trying in vain to come up with a reason for him to stay. She watched him walk to the side of the house and disappear down the path. Moments later she heard the sound of his ball hitting the racquet and then the wall.

Emma lay where she was for another ten minutes or so, but now the sound of his tennis ball was intrusive. Its rhythm kept the image of the young man before her eyes, whether they were closed or open. She tried to think of other things. She tried to recapture the mood she was enjoying before the interruption but nothing would cure her of the strange and uncomfortable malady brought on by his momentary visit.

Once safely inside she was able to chide herself for her foolishness. The boy had fallen from the sky in a moment when she was highly aroused. Her feelings were an accident of circumstances, nothing more. This rationalisation did little to calm her heightened senses. She drank a glass of water and stared out of her kitchen window. Across the side passage was the window of her neighbours' house. She could see right into their rumpus room. The room was empty. There was the pool table she and her husband had played on a few nights before. Would she ever be able to be so comfortable in that house again?

Emma pulled the cord to her Venetian blinds and let the slats fall noisily and heavily down, tidying her view. She wished she could do the same in her mind. Her imagination was building upon the chaste scene she'd just shared with Jason, improving the dialogue, developing the themes and changing the outcome to suit her immodest expectations. The fact that any involvement with him was impossible only made the subject more attractive to the fantasist. The sound of the tennis ball was still audible. With a flick of a switch music filled the room. Pock-pock. She ran upstairs to her bedroom at the front of the house. She changed into her jeans quickly and threw on the top she'd been wearing earlier. But pulling on her jeans had excited her. She was on heat. It was all so unexpected. There was no way around it. The bitch switch had been flicked.

Now, in front of the mirror, she stood studying herself with new eyes. She adjusted her hair and looked closely at her face, pursing her lips then relaxing them into a smile. Her eyes lied to her. They looked calm, indifferent and in control. In a flash the t-shirt she'd just put on came off and with it the bikini top beneath. Her breasts were scrutinised. She'd always liked her breasts, but now she looked at them and wondered whether they were sagging. She lifted them with two hands and let them drop. His youth had rattled her. His body was so vital, youthful, potent. How quickly time seemed to run away from one. It was almost a year since she had married David. She had just turned thirty-two.

Before she knew what she had done she found

herself at the back of the house, in a guest bedroom looking down at the boy hitting the tennis
ball in his backyard. She was still topless, as was
he. She wondered whether he would look up and
catch the crazy old lady next door flashing her
boobs at him.

But Jason was totally absorbed in the task at
hand – which was more adorable than sexy. His
feet moved swiftly and his muscles were sharply
defined as he hit the ball with surprising power.
He seemed taller, stronger and fitter than ever
before but he had a boy's look of concentration.
The ball would rebound from the wall at great
speed and he was there, ready and waiting, nearly
every time. He'd been known to do this all day.
Emma had paid him no attention in the past
except heed the sound of the ball. He'd only ever
been the neighbours' son. But now . . .

Minutes passed by as she watched his graceful
athleticism.

She wandered away from the window, conscious of every step. She seemed helpless against
the onrush of her desire and could barely hold
herself steady. She lay on her bed and tried to
relax, but realised it was the wicked nature of her
desire which had done this to her. He was not just

a handsome young man, he was the neighbours' son. Her lovely, sweet neighbours' nice, polite, naive, handsome son. Their little boy. On this nice street, in this nice neighbourhood in Mosman.

That was the key to her disturbed state. She needed a release. She'd been good for so long. She'd never been married before, she'd never been so restricted in her choice of sexual partners. Her life was once very different. She was not unhappy with her marriage. She loved David. She was surprised by him every day. He was more attentive to her needs than many men would know how to be. David was an instinctual lover, an insatiable man-beast. She was not unhappy, not at all, except in this: she needed from time to time to be very naughty.

TWO

Emma had remained faithful to her husband for three long months. This may not seem long, especially when we note that fidelity in marriage is presumed to be lifelong. But Emma knew the exact quantity of respect, in days, a modern marriage deserves. Eighty-nine days, or roughly three months, was her assessment. This was according to her concentrated personal brand of respect not the heavily diluted brand commonly bandied about.

Her behaviour seemed worse than it was. Her only indiscretions were with her lifelong friend and lover, Paul. Emma was not a bad woman. Morality was the guiding light of her life. She wanted to live by morals that recognised and included who she was – a self-reliant, thinking, sensual woman. She did not need to be protected by archaic moral laws. These did more damage than good. She was not a coward. She'd read widely on the subject of morality and rejected most moral systems as basically sexist. They tended to reflect the supposed needs of women in a world greatly different from the one she found herself in. She did not relate to those traditional moral guidelines. Her own system of values was exact and, she would boast, thoroughly examined. How many of us can declare they have done as much? She was more than ready to defend her moral position against bigots. She had discarded, over time, many values people mistakenly believed, and still believe, to be essential. That was all.

According to Emma's lover, Paul, a three-month hiatus was excessive. Emma was sure she knew best. She'd actually told him she'd remain faithful to her husband till the day she died. This was a bold lie to excite a certain response. Her lover was disconsolate but nevertheless, from her first denial on her wedding day, he redoubled his efforts to seduce her. She was chased round her home and even pinned against the wall when David was in the next room.

Paul was incorrigible. Over weeks he begged, teased, threatened and had come close a number of exhilarating times to resorting to the extreme of taking her by force, but his good heart got the better of him. Emma had always found Paul very attractive, for many reasons, and had indulged his every whim since meeting him in her teens. Denying him now, and by default herself, was a very, very erotic act. To Emma the good life was a life of play.

One night, shortly after Paul had tried his best to tempt Emma in the hallway while David was pouring them champagne in the living room, Paul found himself alone in said living room and distinctly heard the brutish sounds of David reaching climax with his wife, probably in the very same alcove where his own attempt had come to nothing. The smile on Emma's face when she reappeared was worth the searing jealousy Paul had felt and more. She was his devil.

Emma was sure an erotic life must be managed, if only loosely managed. Marriage awakens in oneself, and in others, a wealth of traditional values and habitual perspectives which permeate one's life. People treat a husband or a wife differently.

Living with a man just doesn't have the same status, there is no solidity to it, and therefore no risks are involved if one were to stray or be led astray. In the eyes of a predatory outsider, marriage is a fixed entity which must be acknowledged. The seduction of a married person requires subtle arts not needed at other times.

David was all for their marrying. He thought it the natural progression of their relationship. Emma was the one for him – case closed. She was dead-set against it, until . . . until she discovered the erotic potential of marriage. Then she got married, much like a good girl puts on a pair of sexually charged high heels for the first time. Marriage as an erotic accessory.

Some people may jump to the conclusion that Emma did not love her husband but this would be a hasty judgement, for Emma was unlike most women, or more like their potential, their true selves, than their actual selves. She was a sexual glutton but, like any good diet, her diet required variety.

∞

The faint pock-pock of the tennis ball reached Emma's ear where she lay, in the safety of her bedroom. The very sound had her imagining wicked things. But she was being foolish. She had to distract herself.

The fact was she did have things to do. Important things. She was a first-year student of Literature, History and Philosophy. The bag she used to lug books to and from the library hung from the back of her door. She took it down. She'd been so bad lately, letting the essays pile up. And to think she might have spent the whole day lying in the sun. Where was her laptop? Time was running out. Her first year was nearly complete. As was her first year of marriage, come to think of it.

Where had the year gone?

Pock-pock. Pock-pock.

She stood in the middle of her room listening to the sound.

THREE

When Emma and David first met, a little over a year ago, David had been living out of boxes in an awful one-bedroom flat in North Sydney with no view. His work and social life was so full and demanding he rarely did more than sleep there. Which was why he hadn't bothered to unpack the boxes or to take the plastic off some of the furniture he'd had delivered.

There was no mistaking him, David Benson was a successful man, a man's man. He had few talents but those he had he exploited. He had a head for numbers, was quick with them, and often found himself with a solution before others recognised there was a problem. He was a decision maker in a world of indecision. With David on your side things moved forward at a rapid rate. His bosses recognised this, as did his brighter colleagues. Many rose with him, till David led a tight group of like-minded men who made an enormous amount of money for their masters and for themselves.

David had been squirrelling away his earnings for something inconclusively labelled 'The Future'. For a family, presumably, though it wasn't openly acknowledged as such by him. But life is short and time was draining away faster and faster, and he was thirty-five and hadn't had a steady girlfriend for years.

Before meeting Emma he could make time for sport but would rarely make time for a woman. Business first, above all, then sport.

And then David met Emma.

When Paul, their mutual friend, introduced Emma and David, he did so in the spirit of play. Emma, he believed, would tear down David's 'citadel of bullshit', a shorthand phrase Paul used to describe his friend's belief system. And David would give Emma the shake she needed.

So Paul arranged for them to meet. He chose a bar in the city. A bar he knew David frequented. He wanted David to feel comfortable. He wanted David to be himself. He wanted Emma to meet the David the world saw.

David was late and Paul spent the time preparing Emma for what she was about to receive. But no male can properly describe another male to a female. And when David finally arrived Emma realised Paul had missed one vital point, David's presence. Maybe it was because the men had known each other from childhood but Paul hadn't spoken of David's size. Hadn't mentioned the casual grace with which he held all that power at bay. Emma saw an untapped energy source. A sleeping Leviathan. A barbarian taught to wear a suit and shown how to use a knife and fork. To a woman like Emma this was a man unlike any she had encountered before. All that power and yet, she was quick to note, his eyes told her he had that essential germ necessary for tenderness, empathy. Underneath all the layers of so-called civilisation she could sense the man was intelligent and, more importantly, good.

Having said all that, Emma was responding less to the intelligence report garnered by her mind than she was responding to a thumping physical report proffered by her body.

David too had been quick to appreciate a marked difference between this woman and many of the women he had known in the past. Just the way Emma held his eyes with her own was enough to dismiss the concerns of the day. At first he thought she was defiant but this was wrong. He thought for that moment she was strutting, puffing out her chest in the manner women with hairy armpits, atrocious dress sense and coloured hair at university used to do when he would stumble into the wrong bar.

But he realised his mistake. This woman knew she was easily his equal. He was facing a reversal of fortune for he suddenly realised he was being judged to see if *he* was worthy. And what was worse, he raced to the conclusion that, no, he was not.

He was uncomfortably aware that the mere movement of her lips as she spoke, and how well she spoke, was arousing him more than any lap dancer, any drunk secretary undressing in his office, in fact any erotic encounter in his entire life. She had a natural, easy manner that hid something provocative from him and the world.

She was dazzling him with her words, which he saw dancing around him. She was talking about Tangiers. She was talking about ordering them both Caprioskas. She was asking him about his family and he was answering. But he felt – he was sure of it – he felt her hand on his crotch. He actually had to look to see that it wasn't there. Weren't each of her fine words fingers on a hand which was, this very moment, cradling his cock? Such suggestiveness he'd never known.

He thought her the most beautiful, the most attractive woman he had ever met.

The couple were married in under two months of Paul's orchestrated meeting.

It was one thing to know when a person is *the one*, it is another thing to live with them. Both Emma and David had enjoyed very independent lives. Emma had always seen to it that she was able to afford to live alone. David had always expected he'd eventually have a large home to call his own. Emma never had such grandiose expectations. Marrying David was an experience akin to stepping into a parallel universe and not being able to leave.

The trouble with stepping into a parallel universe is that from now on there would always be two 'yous' to deal with. And this Emma discovered very soon after marrying.

She kept the old life going. She couldn't, or wilfully wouldn't, let it go. She needed to be independent Emma and married Emma at the same time, even though each had mutually exclusive agendas.

The very idea of sharing a life with someone seemed to her to be impossible. It *had* seemed possible before marriage, but we know how practical a theory can seem before testing. Now it was impossible.

She loved David. She wanted to be with David. She wanted to wake beside him. But just as his business life excluded her completely, her independent life necessarily excluded him. He worked long hours, still played lots of sport and was very social. What right had he to know what she did during all that time? None. Just because he chose to spend his time in a socially acceptable manner didn't change the fact that during that time she was out of his mind completely. He just used his time unwisely. Emma had the right idea.

A week after Emma's flirtation with Jason from next door she was sitting on her balcony with David, her head nestled on his shoulder, wondering how she could keep feeling sexy with a husband who demanded so little from her. She felt in herself a massive potential for fun.

They'd just made love. These moments were lovely, spontaneous and dangerous in a very limited sense of the word. The neighbours were unlikely to spy them where they lay. She liked these times. But they fed some other part of her needs, not her erotic needs. Her erotic needs seemed so vast by comparison to those warm and fuzzy regions which lapped up tenderness. A shoulder to lie on, a warm body spooning her, hugs, kisses, caresses and comfort were an essential part of love and easily satisfied. David appeared to be completely happy with their sex life.

The sex *was* great. That wasn't the problem. The life outside the sex was the problem.

She had lived a wonderfully erotic life which was separate from her marriage. She could not find a way to combine them both. And as her need to lie developed she was aware that the window of opportunity for change was closing.

The trouble was, the more she loved David the harder it became to hurt him. She wanted to share her erotic life with him, to open up to him about her sexual life and convince him that to share in her experiences was to truly know her and be included in a much wider sexual world. She hated to think that little hurts would forever keep half her life from him. The fun half. The upshot was, however, that in the last year, in order not to hurt her husband, the door to her erotic life had all but closed.

By the third week of her conscientious effort to complete all that she had to complete for university Emma realised she had been a little foolish in some of her recent behaviour. She had been avoiding the back garden. Temptations, however slight, were to be avoided, it would seem. Without commenting internally on her choices, she had chosen to sit on her bedroom balcony high above the street, with a book or her computer, at the same time each afternoon. Jason never noticed her sitting there when he came home and Emma made no outward sign of noticing him. Temptation was at bay, but the interest was still there, simmering perhaps . . . perhaps not.

FOUR

Another day, another idle hour and another chance to lay out one's towel while the sun shone on the square of grass in the backyard. Emma had recommenced her practice of spending part of her day bikini-clad bathing in the sun's brilliance. For the last week when the weather was fine she would stop working away at her essays to take a short recess. Most days she would read while lying stretched out on her towel, revisiting old favourites.

Ever since young Jason had leapt over the fence Emma had been in the habit of reminiscing and as books were like milestones on her path into her past she had been interested in re-reading some of the most influential.

Re-reading the erotic stories of Anaïs Nin, Emma was less impressed by the stories than by the memories they conjured up. Past lovers were before her eyes again. Each passing man had served to disillusion her in some way. But reading the stories she was able, for a time, to feel what it was to have such grand expectations. She was able to relive, to a certain extent, the excitement she felt before the curtain of experience had come down. She wanted to feel such heightened emotions again.

When she thought of what her first few lovers had shared, when she considered them from the point of view of an adult, she was astonished at how powerfully the experiences had affected her. And how she, she now knew, had affected the men. What it must have been like for them, especially the much older men, the risks they were taking, she only now considered and these considerations made her past appear all the more erotic.

One moment in particular stood out. An older man. A neighbour. A married man. The first time he had touched her – undoing her pants in a public place, a car park, thrilling her to almost unbearable levels, paralysing her body and mind – was a moment she might live but once. She would never again experience the uncertainty, she would never feel the anticipation or the bewilderment at those extreme levels again.

When Emma sat up to reapply her suncream she became aware of a familiar sound – the pock-pock of a tennis ball on the back wall of her neighbours' house. The sound alone was enough to make her whole body tingle. She marvelled at herself for not noticing the sound earlier.

Sitting cross-legged she rubbed the cream in her skin and listened. She had come to recognise that the circumstances which led to his sudden appearance were rather extraordinary. He was, by his parents' own account, a very good boy and so by skipping school that day he had been acting against type. The sound of the tennis ball now seemed to suggest otherwise. There was nothing special about this particular Monday afternoon that she knew of.

The pock-pock of the tennis ball was not as inarticulate as one might have expected. To Emma the sound spoke volumes. She rubbed the cream into her legs, running her hand all the way down her shin to her bare foot, thinking all the while of her neighbour's lean torso twisting as he hit the tennis ball. She convinced herself that this sound was not an accident. Very few accidents have their sequel.

He had taken the day off to speak with her.

Then a bright green tennis ball had fallen squarely in her view, in the middle of the lawn. The ball had landed gently, as if placed, she was quick to note. She lay down on her stomach and waited.

She did not wait long. Hearing a grunt she raised her eyes to the top of the boundary fence. Jason flung himself over it with all the poise of a gymnast dismounting from the parallel bars. He smiled sheepishly at Emma then tried to pretend he was surprised to see her lying there. He had looked far more comfortable accomplishing that first feat of leaping the fence than this second one. Acting was not going to be his forte.

'Young Master Singer! What a surprise!' said Emma, raising her head slightly.

'I didn't know you were home. I mishit my ball. Have you seen it?' said Jason, hurrying through his lines. They sounded as spontaneous as the chanted responses at a funeral service.

'Relax, honey, there's your ball,' she said coolly. She lay her head down as if that was that.

Jason did not move. She could sense his confusion. This was all very awkward. Unnecessarily so. What she wanted to do was put him at his ease. He was much cuter when he wasn't trying so hard.

She had noted with some excitement that he was wearing nothing but his board shorts again. She couldn't find her responsible adult hat today. She had looked at him while he was speaking with predatory intent. But he was so young. There would be no satisfaction without restraint, without timing.

Emma opened her eyes and spied his feet through her eyelashes. He was stuck in the centre of her lawn.

'Is it a holiday today?' she asked, coming to his rescue.

'No, it's a home study day,' he lied.

'A what?' she laughed, raising her head and looking directly at him. 'Liar.'

'No, really, it is,' he said.

'Shall I ring your mum's shop to find out if she knows about your home study day?'

'Can if you like,' he said, easily. He was more proficient in this kind of banter.

'Calling my bluff, huh?' she said, and patted the ground in front of her.

'I knew you wouldn't call,' he said. 'You're too nice.'

'Am I?'

'Yes.'

'Or do you think I'm a pushover?'

'No!'

'Do you mind that I think you're cute?' she asked, in her usual teasing manner.

He made no reply, which was his usual response. She patted the grass in front of her again, and he plonked down this time, legs crossed, elbows on his knees holding the ball in his cupped hands. He sat facing her and her breasts. She reached across and tried to take the ball but he was too fast. She let her hand rest on his knee. She left it there.

'Do you want a drink?' she asked.

'Yeah,' he said.

'So would I.' She lay back down and closed her eyes.

'You want me to get them?' he said, jumping up.

'Yep, there's beer in the fridge,' she said. He tossed the tennis ball back over the fence and dashed inside.

He was always moving quickly. He had so much energy.

FIVE

Jason returned with a bottle of beer for Emma and a glass of water for himself.

'You can have one of these. I won't tell,' she said, taking the beer as he offered it to her. She wouldn't normally drink a beer. She knew she was angling now.

'I don't drink much,' he said.

'God you're straight. I was a dope fiend at your age.' She lay her head down again.

'I just don't feel like it,' he said.

'One beer never killed anybody. But hey, if you don't want one . . .'

She was silent. He stood feeling awkward, not knowing whether to sit on the grass or the chair. Or whether it would be best to leave. He sensed that Emma was in a weird mood. There was something strange in the air. He thought she was sad about something. He wasn't comfortable with adult sadness.

He was wrong though. Emma wasn't sad.

'Your mum tells me you've got a girlfriend,' she said.

Jason almost spat water everywhere.

'I haven't,' he said, after he had coughed.

'She said you were hanging out with Jess.'

'I don't even know a Jess,' he lied.

'What do you do with her?'

'Nothing,' he said.

'Have you *done it* with her?'

He was silent. Emma smiled at him.

'Have I offended you?'

'No.'

'Are you a virgin?'

'I'm eighteen,' he said in an unconvincingly indignant tone, still standing. He looked very nervous. Then she noticed the bulge in his pants. She saw that he had tucked the tip of his penis under the strap of his boxers to keep it hidden. He must have done it when he went for the drinks. All it did was highlight the long shape of his erection. That's why he was standing. God, that's cute, she thought. Then she wondered what it was that gave him the erection. Well, what it was *exactly*.

'Look, Jason. Go grab yourself a beer and come back and keep me entertained. It's hours before David will be home.'

Jason was happy for the excuse to go. He stood in the kitchen trying, in vain, to take control of his embarrassing condition. He worried about taking the beer, but reconsidered when he remembered that it was Monday. His parents usually came home later on Monday. His dad played squash and his mum had a cookery class.

He reached in the fridge and grabbed the glass bottle. He opened it and tossed the cap in the bin. He took a swig and released the obligatory 'Ahhh' then hurried out to Emma.

He sat on the grass beside her. Her face was turned from him so he had time to arrange his erection so that it looked normal.

'What are you doing home anyway?' she asked, still facing away from him.

'I'm not,' he replied.

'So you're at school.'

'Yep.'

'Definitely not here drinking a beer with me.'

'That's right.'

'Oh, that's how it is, huh?' she said and turned her head so as to face him. 'Am I meant to keep it secret?'

'Yes,' he said, taking a long swig of beer.

'What do I get in return?'

'Nothing.'

'I don't know if I like the way you bargain,' she said, closing her eyes.

'You said you were bored.'

'I am never bored. I have too many good memories to mull over, and then there are my wicked plans . . . How can I be bored?'

'You're weird.' He put the bottle down on the path which ran just to the left of him.

'Don't you like me?' she asked, raising herself and lying on her side, propping her head up with her arm. Jason was gazing at her body. He caught her catching him and looked away.

'I like you, but you are weird.'

'Do you like the way I look?' she asked.

'Yes,' he said, picking up his bottle again, and turning it this way then that in his hands. Relieving the bottle of its label became the one important act of his life. His fingernails found the edge.

'Have you thought about me?' she asked.

'What do you mean?' His eyes lowered. He lifted the entire length of the label's edge.

'You know what I mean.'

'Nup,' he said. He looked up at the eucalypt.

'You don't think about me?'

'No,' he said smiling. The label ripped.

'I've thought about you,' she said.

He went bright red. Tore shreds of the label from the bottle.

'Look, Jason, I don't want to frighten you . . .'

'You're not!' he said shrilly, before taking a sip of beer to steady the scene while surreptitiously rolling the fragments of label between his thumb and forefinger.

'Do you think I'm old?' she asked, genuinely interested, because it occurred to her that he might think of her as she used to think of her parents' friends when she was young.

Suddenly it was Emma's turn to be embarrassed. She had answered her own question before he had even understood it, imagining him shaking his head condescendingly. Of course he would think she was old.

'How old *are* you?' he asked. This was his real reaction. He flicked the paper balls over her.

'So you *do* think I'm old?' she said, feeling her vanity and her surety shake.

'You're married. I mean. I don't know.'

'I'm twenty-three,' she said, lying.

'That's not bad,' he said, not knowing whether it was bad or good or what. He desperately wanted her to change the subject.

'Do I look old to you?' she asked.

'Yes,' he said, in that honesty which comes from not knowing what to say.

'Really?'

'You're married! And . . .'

'Is my body unattractive?'

Jason sighed in relief. He was on safe ground again.

'Your body is very attractive,' he said, calmly, though he had yet to look her in the eye for more than a millisecond the whole time they'd been talking. He drank some of his beer.

'But I'm old looking?'

'You're older than Jess,' he said, getting nervous again.

'She's sixteen, for Christ sakes. Of course I am!'

'That's what I meant,' he said.

'So I'm only old with regard to Jess but other than that I'm fine?'

'I don't know.'

'What?'

'I can't say.'

'Tell me,' she said, leaning across and touching his leg, again.

He shook his head.

'Come on,' she coaxed.

'Well, it's not easy to say.' He started to peel away a large shred of label.

'What?'

'You really want to know?' he said. The piece of label came away from the bottle.

'Yes,' she said, 'it's okay, you can tell me anything. I want us to be good friends. No secrets.'

'OK.' He rolled that piece too.

'Well?' she said, rubbing his leg unnecessarily.

'Her breasts . . .' He stopped, tongue tied. She waited.

'Yes?' she asked, realising he wouldn't go on.

'Hers are firm.' He looked down.

'Ha!' she laughed. 'She hasn't got any! Ha ha! I thought . . .'

'What?'

'I thought you were going to say something about my arse or my wrinkles or fat or something,' she said, still giggling.

'You haven't got any wrinkles.'

'I know that! But I am fat and my arse wobbles though, right?'

'I didn't say that. Nothing is wrong with your body,' he said, desperately trying to stop himself from sinking for good.

'You're so cute. I want to eat you all up!' She squeezed his leg.

He was silent, red faced and happy. He flicked this tiny ball over her too.

'But my tits are saggy?' she said suddenly.

His mouth opened wide about to defend himself again when she leaped over and bit him on the thigh.

She growled. He pretended that it didn't hurt. She shook like a crocodile and clawed him for good measure.

She pushed him over and her hand accidentally ran the full length of his erection. She growled some more and then lay on her back.

'I'm going to BBQ you one day,' she said casually, as though her spirited attack had never happened.

'Your breasts aren't saggy,' he said, sitting back up. He watched the teeth marks she'd left on his inner thigh turn red. There was some pain but he was more aware of an impulse within him which he likened to moments he had had when fighting in the school yard. These fights were rough, very physical ordeals which erupted from petty misunderstandings or idiotic questions of pride. He found he gravitated towards them more than ever. Sometimes, in the midst of a rumble, he would face some irrational impulse to perform some greater and more satisfying act. The impulse to do this indefinite something was so strong and he felt it with his entire body. As this impulse thumped round him he looked at her face, then breasts, her naked belly, at her bikini bottoms and the mound they hid and down her smooth white legs, at her ankles and her toes.

'I know they're not saggy,' she said, sitting up and crossing her legs. 'Do you want to see them?'

He thought she was teasing so he said, 'No.' His body stopped thumping. He went cold. His pride pricked up its ears.

'Oohh, why not?' She bent her torso over her crossed legs, showing herself to be flexible, and took his right hand in her two hands. She brought it to her lips and kissed the back of it.

'Why do you always tease me?' he asked. 'It's not fair.'

'It's because I like you,' she said, kissing the tips of his fingers one by one.

SIX

Jason watched her silently and felt the warmth of her mouth on his fingers. The feeling was unlike any he had known. *Better* than anything he had known. Then she took his thumb into her mouth and sucked on it. He watched her, stunned. His erection throbbed but he was terrified.

'Why do you lie in the sun if you wear 30+?' he asked. The question just occurred to him.

'I don't like tans but I love the heat. It makes me feel completely relaxed. I love the sun,' she answered, interrupting her play, but not raising herself.

She began to suck his thumb again. Then released it and said, 'I'll read you a story by D.H. Lawrence called "Sun" one day if you'd like. I don't like his writing much but that particular story is yummy.'

He ignored these words or, more to the point, they were gibberish to him and didn't require attention. As soon as she stopped speaking she began sucking his thumb again.

'I like your skin,' he said.

She kept sucking, she was heating up. She stopped and replied, 'Thank you. Jess is very brown. Who do you like better?'

'I like you better,' he said.

'Good.' Then she turned his hand over and began to kiss his palm, letting her tongue circle around, reading it and predicting his future.

'That feels nice,' he said.

'What does Jess do to you?'

'We haven't even kissed,' he said.

'Really? Why not?'

'I think we're only friends.'

'You know I'm friends with her mother, don't you? I know Jess well.'

'No!' he said. How could she be?

She licked his palm and then his wrist and then lifted her face from it to say, 'We talked about you.'

'What did she say?'

'I can't tell you that.'

'Come on, please.'

'I want you for my own,' she said.

He was silent. He wanted so desperately to know whether she was joking or not. He hated being made fun of.

'You want both of us, don't you?'

'No,' he said. 'Just you.'

She smiled brightly at him. She felt like a teenager again. She was really falling for him. He was so eager to please and eager not to offend.

'You're about to do your final exams, right?' she asked, knowing that he was but she was trying to feel the full force of what she was about to propose.

'Yep. In a few weeks. Then I'm done with school forever.'

'You can't let yourself be distracted then?'

'No.'

'Do you think it's wrong for me to like you?'

'Yes,' he said. He was nothing if not guileless. Subconsciously he was readying himself for a fall. In one quick movement she could fake with her right and knock him flat with her left. He left himself open for her. It was something like

45

masturbating behind an unlocked door when you knew it was too risky to do so. The prospect of further pleasure can make one brave and stupid. It was unlikely that Emma would be genuinely attracted to him so as the seconds ticked by he tried to convince himself that he was reading this all wrong – she wasn't interested in him, she couldn't be.

'I like that it is wrong. Do you?'

'No,' he said.

She reached over and stroked his cock.

'Well I do. It *is* wrong, you know. I shouldn't do this to you. It isn't fair, I know. I should act responsibly. You're young. I know your parents. If anything should happen. I mean, if anyone should find out.'

'You're acting all crazy!' he said, shrilly.

'Can I kiss you?' she asked.

He didn't acknowledge her.

'Can I? Huh?'

She leant further forward, uncrossing her legs and kneeling. She put her hand on his knee and leant on it, bringing her face close to his. She was about to kiss him when she came to think of his feelings. It wasn't for the first time either. She wasn't a monster. If he had been a young girl she would have been far gentler. Once you get going with a boy or a man for that matter, it is easy to disregard their feelings, dumb beasts that they are.

She paused, their faces hovering an inch apart in suspended animation.

He moved forward and the soft skin of his fleshy lips brushed ever so lightly against her own.

'I'm sorry, Jason, but I can't do it,' she said, making no move to end the closeness. His lips brushed hers again. 'I mean, I *want* to do it. I so want to kiss you and do other stuff besides but . . .'

'What?' he whispered. Here comes her left hook. Duck!

'What?'

'Yeah, what?' he said.

She crawled up over him and sat in his lap, wrapping her legs around his back and pressing her whole body against him. She felt his hard cock against her and the warm skin of his abdomen against her own. She squeezed him with all her might and he gasped.

'If you say I'm old again I'll squeeze you to death,' she said through clenched teeth. He laughed and she brought her mouth against his, rushing when she might take it slow. The pressure of his young cock up against her like that was making her lose her restraint. She wanted so much to have him slip into her. To fuck him as they were. She imagined squeezing herself around his cock and grinding herself against him over and over. These thoughts made her wet and she ached for his fingers or cock or, she thought with a shiver, his inexperienced tongue to penetrate her.

She kissed him with closed mouth and then gave him little kisses down his cheek until she reached the base of his neck, and she kissed his swimmer's shoulders, biting into the salty flesh and making him moan involuntarily into her ear.

She never wanted to stop. She bit him and kissed him up and down and then returned to his mouth. She parted his lips with her tongue and his tongue hid from her. She searched for it, looking and tasting and feeling her way around his mouth. Then she found his warm tongue and coaxed it out and danced with it. She felt his strong tongue enter her mouth and she sucked on it. He began to flick it in and out and she bit down lightly on it and held it and sucked it.

His hands lay limp beside him and she picked them up in her own and brought them round to her hips. They gripped her and squeezed her and she moaned dramatically.

He started to rub his hands all over her back and she had shivers and goose bumps that ran all the way through her. He clutched the back of her neck and forced her closer to him. The dull pressure of this made their kiss insistent and teased the hunger each felt for the other. Jason's hunger was indefinite, diffuse and this made it greater than any hunger he had ever felt. His was a crater which no sensation could fill. Hers was definite, chiselled, precise; a sharp pang that might wake you from sleep.

Emma lifted her butt so that his cock came to rest on her clitoris. Without letting on that she was being self-serving she managed to rub herself against him. The pressure was gorgeous to her, it began to feed her hunger and she kissed his mouth passionately. Her bikini bottoms were wet. He rubbed against her. She kissed his mouth and timed her movements, pressing then releasing her clitoris against his cock.

Soon, sooner than she had expected, the thrill of an orgasm overcame her and she tensed up, pushing her face against his, kissing him deeply in return for his own deep kisses. She felt the need to hide her pleasure from him. She tried to control her moans and her shakes. But she needn't have worried. Jason was ignorant of what had just happened. He was delirious. His dreams of Emma were realised and he was too terrified and aroused to make any judgements.

They kissed like this for near on an hour. Fumbling and rubbing and biting lips and sucking tongues and earlobes and necks. Emma had not done this for years. He made no effort to move things along. He made no effort to touch her breasts or to explore beyond the fleshy butt that he gripped and kneaded so enthusiastically through her bikini bottoms. Jason made no attempt to undress the little Emma had on. He moaned and yet never thought to thrust up.

Emma was not so restrained. She didn't rip his shorts off and beg to be fucked, nor did she direct his hands between her legs, nor did she knock him on his back and gobble up his cock, but she did use it, still enclosed within his board shorts, to get herself off. She came, moaning into his mouth but still managing to keep him blissfully unaware about just how much his naive lovemaking was doing to her.

Emma slowed things down. She kissed his face with beautiful little kisses. She kissed his eyelids. She kissed his brow. She moved off him. She was stiff and sore after an hour in the one position but she laughed when Jason revealed that he couldn't move.

'My legs have gone to sleep,' he said, smiling, his face one of blissed out serenity.

'Something hasn't gone to sleep,' she said, glancing at the tent of his board shorts. She laughed when she saw that his tent was wet, and she looked down and realised that her bikini bottoms were drenched.

'Sorry,' she said, 'that was my fault.'

He looked at her strangely.

'You made me so wet, Jason. Haven't you done that to a girl before?'

'No. I haven't done anything.'

'Really? Oh shit. I am a bad woman.'

'Yes,' he said shyly.

'We are going to have so much fun together,' she said, kissing him again. She left him alone and sat on her butt. Somewhere in her mind a plan was forming. It was forming in direct opposition to all her immediate desires. These desires wanted her to run through the whole *Kama Sutra* with him in one afternoon. But her plans said, 'No!'

Emma gripped him through the shorts. He

moaned. After a few strokes she knew he was close, very close.

'Emma!' he said, and then he moaned and repeated, 'Emma.'

She wanked him, kneeling in front of him now, thinking of that cock she hadn't even seen, the cock which had made her come twice now.

She wanted to unbutton his shorts and blow him and send him to heaven. But she restrained herself and limited herself to this one simple deed.

She looked at his face and he returned her gaze.

'Emma,' he said. 'Emma!'

He couldn't tell her. He was so unsure.

His strained face was so cute to Emma, so confused and so tense, as it was. She was turned on by his simple pleas. She rubbed his cock and thought of the first time she'd come with another person. She remembered she was so turned on that in the end it took her forever to finally come. She believed it to be the best and most exquisite orgasm she ever had.

And now she was sharing Jason's first-with-another-person. He was so close. Emma could tell.

Rubbing his cock through the shorts Emma

watched every change in his face. His mouth opened and closed. He seemed embarrassed to come in front of her, hadn't realised that it was OK. The pleasure of it, for him, was extreme. The more he held on, held his orgasm back, the more turned on Emma became, the harder her grip, the faster her strokes.

'Emma!' he said again. 'Oh, Emma!'

He was so ready to come.

'Emma!' he said, and a sob escaped and she realised that he was distressed. He was crying.

'Oh baby,' she said, kissing him, 'I want you to come. I want it. Come, baby, don't worry. I want you to come.'

Jason looked at her sheepishly but his pride had no time to assert itself because at that moment the first wave of come shot up his cock and he convulsed, then came another and another. His face showed the strain of orgasm and her hand moved faster and he convulsed again and again. He made no noise. Not a peep.

He collapsed on his back.

'Emma!' he mumbled.

She jumped over and lay on top of him and kissed his face and neck. His limp hands rested on the small of her back.

'Yum, yum, yum, yum, yum,' she said, between each kiss. 'Yum, yum, yum, yum!'

He smiled but was too tired and too relieved to make a sound. He closed his eyes and sighed.

'I want to do it every afternoon,' she said.

His smiled broadened.

SEVEN

A few days later Emma caught sight of Jason as he returned from school. She waved to him and he jogged over. She was standing by her car, heading to the shops. That was, before she caught sight of Jason.

He looked shy and embarrassed.

'Hi,' he said. He waited on the other side of the car and smiled nervously over it.

'Hi there yourself,' she replied, lifting up her sunglasses and placing them on the top of her head. He smiled. And then smiled again.

She locked the car and took a couple of steps

towards her front door then she turned and looked at him again.

'Coming?' she asked, before walking through the gate, up the path, stopping on the verandah before the front door.

She unlocked it and stepped inside.

Jason followed her as quickly as he could and then paused at the threshold.

One. Two. Three. Four. Five. Six.

Jason stepped through the door, waiting for some sign from Emma. He looked down the hall and into the front living room but he couldn't see her.

He stood in the hallway shaking. His felt light-headed. Weak. The anxieties of the last few days came flooding in. He hadn't been able to meet her as they had planned. He had stood her up. He had forgotten that he had cricket training after school. It was the worst afternoon's cricket he had ever played. All he could think of, all he had thought of since Emma's last kiss, was Emma and what she had done to him; what she had said, what she'd promised. But after missing that first afternoon he was sure he had blown it.

The following day he had arrived home from school and Emma's car wasn't out front. Later, when he saw that her car was again parked in front of her house, he was unable to find a credible reason why he would go to Emma's place alone.

But now he was there. He was inside her house where it was cool and quiet. He had no idea what would eventuate. The way Emma had looked at him had made him hard and edgy.

'Where are you, Emma?' he called out down the hall.

'Here,' was her reply from some distant place.

Jason followed the sound of her voice, climbing the stairs. He came to the door he believed was her bedroom. His mind raced. He felt sick to the stomach. He was so nervous. He imagined her lying on her bed beckoning him to her. Suddenly he felt truly frightened. He wanted so much to be something special, to be a good lover for Emma, but her every action, her manner, her confidence and her obvious knowledge made his whole body quiver in tiny, near paralysing twitches. Being in her house, bringing with him the knowledge of the other day, made him nearly blind with pleasure and fear.

Jason stood in the hall. All he could see was the open door. He saw nothing of what was within. He listened and heard Emma moving in the room.

He was just about to make a move forward, over-whelmed by his fear and anxiety and what might happen, when Emma bounded out of the room, making him jump. It was dumb luck rather than a conscious effort that made the scream he released soundless.

'Oh, baby! Did I frighten you?'

'No,' he said, 'I knew you were coming.'

Emma humoured him and took him by the hand.

'Let's watch a movie,' she said. 'It's a favourite of mine.'

Emma dragged Jason along and downstairs before his mind had time to adjust to the new situation.

She saw him looking at her. She had changed into a sarong and wore a short t-shirt which left her midriff naked.

'I like to be comfortable when I watch films. You don't mind, do you? I mean we are friends now, right?'

'Yes,' he said.

'I love the way you don't talk much,' she said, having led him into the lounge room. She pushed him onto the couch.

He smiled as he landed.

'What's the movie?' he asked.

'Wait and see,' she said. 'It's one you'll like.'

She inserted the disc. Jason looked up at her as she turned to him. She stepped over to him, picked up the remote and then fell gracelessly onto the sofa beside him. She smiled across at him.

'Don't I get a kiss?' she said.

'Oh, yes. You're so beautiful,' he added, regretting the words as he spoke them and frowned.

'Thank you, Jason. You're a sweetie.'

Both Emma and Jason sat dead still a foot apart while Emma tried to maintain her composure. She had let herself be seduced by his youth and inexperience. She felt that everything he did was adorable. She wanted to bite him, on his thigh, on his neck, on his butt – she wanted to eat him up entirely.

She shot a sideways glance at him and saw his neck and his worried face and almost cried at how cute they were to her. She felt herself becoming hysterical and tried to calm herself. She had such delicious plans for him and she didn't want to waste his unique and fleeting youth and naivety in one great orgy of sensation. If he touched her now, she thought, it would be all over. She'd have his cock out in a flash and would have his untrained body lying heavily upon her as he thrust into her with thudding and inexperienced lunges. Then she thought that he might lose patience with her and she became wet at the idea of his naked aggression pinning her down.

'Are you alright?' asked Jason, full of concern.

'I'm fine, just fine,' she said.

Emma brought his face to her own and for the first time since they'd parted in the backyard she felt his soft lips against hers. His tongue jutted out and she bit it softly and tamed it. She lulled his sweet mouth back into her power. She thought of the daydreams he must have had about her in the time they were separated and this increased her pleasure. She wanted to have him on her. She wanted the simple weight of him. But she held off. She kissed him away from her. He went to speak but she stopped him with her mouth and then let her hand drift down and she felt the hard mound in his jeans.

'Fuck!' she said, and then let go and moved away, picking up the remote control again.

'Movie time,' she said.

Jason was an open book. His face dropped and a little hint of anger could be seen on his good-looking countenance.

'Don't you want to watch my film?'

'No,' he said, suddenly forthright and obviously pleased with himself for being so.

'That's fine. We can just talk. I don't mind. Really I don't.'

Jason looked apprehensive.

'It's like you're playing with me,' he said. 'I'm not dumb. You can treat me the same as anyone else.'

'I know that. Jason, don't get angry with me.'

'I'm not angry.'

She looked at him, forcing her bottom lip out, feigning a sad face. 'Come on. Let's be friends again.'

'Emma, I love you!'

'Good! I love you too, darling.'

'No! I really do,' he said.

'No. You want to fuck me,' she said, and when she saw his face cloud over with a confused and worried storm she leant towards him and took both his hands in hers and said, 'It's true. It is and I don't mind. You don't have to tell me you love me. You don't. I want to fuck you. I really do and I will. I will fuck you and more. But I need things to go slow. I don't like to be rushed. Let's just take things as they come. OK?'

Jason seemed happy with this; he nodded at her

every word. It was as if some dread, some barrier had been lifted.

'Were you worried?' Emma asked, having suddenly struck upon an idea.

'Yes.'

'What about?'

'I was just worried,' he said.

'Well now you don't have to be worried. Think of me as . . .'

They were silent.

'My mistress?' he asked, smiling and still looking straight ahead.

'Yes. Yes. I am your mistress. But with one difference, I make all the rules. OK?'

'OK.'

Emma was devising a plan. She thought of herself as his teacher not his mistress. She would teach him to be the lover she had always longed to meet.

Trouble was, teachers had patience, self-restraint, and Jason had the power to strip Emma of both.

'Now go home and think about what I've said.'

Jason turned his face to her. 'But . . .'

'But nothing . . . Where were you Tuesday afternoon? And yesterday?'

'I had training,' he said.

'Well you should have told me,' she said. 'I waited here in my bikini all afternoon and you were nowhere.'

'I'm sorry, Emma, but . . .'

'I'm kidding. It's okay. I don't mind. But you have to go home. Think of it as training for the future. You can't get away with standing up a woman, whatever the excuse. Now go.'

Jason rose. He looked confused again.

'I still want to kiss you and mess with you but you have to wait until tomorrow afternoon.'

'I have training,' he said.

'Skip it!' She looked up at him, watched him check her out. His eyes were the only part of him which revealed to her how much he hungered for her and her resolve wavered under their gaze.

'What do you want?' she asked after he had stood over her for a minute or so.

'I want . . .' He dropped to his knees and threw his arms around her, bringing his lips to hers.

She accepted his advances for a moment before repulsing them.

'Go home, Jason.'

'But . . .' He took her hand in his and kissed the back of it before turning it over and kissing the palm.

'You smoothie,' she said, smiling.

He grinned.

'Home,' she whispered.

'No,' he whispered back.

'David will be home soon,' she lied.

'No, he won't.'

'Yes, he will.'

'You were going to watch a movie with me,' he said.

'How clever you are.'

He smiled.

'Now go home because I say so!' she said, giving him one last kiss and a squeeze on the bum.

She saw his hard-on pressed against his jeans.

'Take that home,' she said.

He blushed at this. The idea of masturbating still seemed so shocking a topic of conversation to him that he turned bright red.

'Fuck! Jason! We all do it. One day I might do it in front of you. Would you like that?'

He shook his head.

'We'll see,' she said. 'Run along. Go on, get out of here.'

Jason turned and left before Emma had expected him to. She lay back on the sofa and let out a huge sigh.

EIGHT

Emma stood on the sand in the morning sun-shine, arms crossed against her chest. She wore her one-piece swimming costume, her hair was tied up in a bun and her goggles dangled from her little finger. The idea was to have her first swim of the season.

But the first touch of the water had stopped her in her tracks. Stranded on the water's edge she felt a fool. Others were walking down to the lapping waves and striding in, diving under the surface to rise ready to begin their laps across the bay.

Holding her hand up to shield her eyes from

the low morning sun she counted twenty or so swimmers out there already. The longer she hesitated the more childish she felt. She just could not turn back. On her way down to the water she had passed all of the early morning coffee drinkers, the loungers and soft sand runners. To turn back now would be a public humiliation. Or so it felt to her.

She tested the water again with her toe. It bit her. Her whole body shivered. There was no going back and there was no going in.

'Emma.'

Someone was calling her name. She turned and scanned the beach and the esplanade. A tanned male raised his arm, leapt over the wall onto the sand and came jogging up to her.

'I thought it was you. Are you going in?'

Jason wore nothing but Speedos which had a pair of goggles hanging from them. There was not an ounce of fat on him.

'I was.'

'Is it too cold for you, Mrs Benson?' he asked, instinctively reverting to the formal. She looked like Mrs Benson today. Was it because her hair was up? Or was it the one-piece? She seemed very pale here on the beach.

Jason stepped into the water. He scrunched up his face and hopped from one foot to the other, mimicking a child, before falling backwards into the water. He leapt straight back up. 'Arrgghh! You're right! It's freezing!'

She smiled. Jason's sudden confidence reminded her of the boys at school who were all rough and tumble with an audience, who would throw her over their shoulder in the spirit of fun, but would go limp when they had the opportunity to touch her.

He strode out of the water and shook himself like a dog.

Emma leapt back as water sprayed from his hair.

'Jason! You bugger!'

'Aren't you going to say hello, Emma?' he asked, holding out his arms as though to hug her. She was about to move away when he caught hold of her hand and began dragging her towards the water.

'Don't you dare!' she shrieked, digging her heels into the sand. 'Don't.'

She had two concerns. She did not want to be tossed into the freezing water, for one. But she was also acutely conscious of how their play would look. The disparity of their ages meant little to her in private, but out here, in public, it felt different. She felt old.

But he had her in his grip. She could see that he gave no thought to how things looked. He was a puppy, lost to the game. She was being dragged in.

'No!'

Her feet touched the water. It was so cold.

He was grinning. He was going to do it.

'Jason, leave poor Emma alone.'

Jason let go and Emma fell backwards onto the sand.

Jason's father, Simon, stretched out his hand and lifted Emma to her feet. He too wore nothing but Speedos. The effect was altogether different to that of his son.

'You have to come in, Mrs Benson,' said Jason, who had wandered back into the water and knelt down.

Now that she was safe, she found it hard to take her eyes off him. He was a near perfect specimen. If anything was going to get her into the water it was the desire to run her hands over his abdomen.

'We were about to swim a few laps, Emma. Will you join us?'

'I was, but it's so cold. I'll try again in a couple of weeks.'

'You should have been here two weeks ago,' called Jason from the water. 'Right, Dad?'

'It's much warmer this week than it has been,' he affirmed.

'Come on.' Jason slapped the water and sent a spray towards Emma which stopped just short of her.

He did it again. He stood up. Emma's eyes drifted slowly down the whole of his body. The Speedos left little to the imagination.

He kicked the water this time.

Emma needed to jump back.

'We've got to get going. Jason has to be at school early this morning. They've organised extra tutoring for Economics. We all believe he's a chance at topping the state. He hasn't got long now before the exams start.' Simon paused and smiled. 'Are you sure you won't come in?' He rinsed his goggles in the water before putting them on.

'Can't. Too cold.'

'OK. We'll see you tonight then.' Simon strode into the water without hesitation.

'Tonight?'

'You and David are coming to dinner. Didn't he tell you?'

Simon dived under the water.

Emma remained standing at the water's edge. She watched as they swam out to start their laps, then turned around and began the ignominious walk back to her towel.

Entering her neighbours' house that evening with David, Emma couldn't shake the tune of Simon and Garfunkel's 'Mrs Robinson'. Jason's antics on the beach had underlined the difference in their ages. He was a boy in a man's body. And now she was entering his parents' house with her husband. It couldn't have become more ridiculous.

Jason was nowhere to be seen. David and Simon drifted off together leaving Emma with Anne for the first twenty minutes, which was fine. Anne was happy to talk pleasantly about the coming and goings of shared acquaintances. She filled the kitchen with noise without noticing Emma's boredom.

'Here he is, my little genius,' said Anne, interrupting her flow as Jason entered the room. She pulled him to her and he tried to escape her arms. 'But he's not so little any more, is he?'

Jason stared at Emma, his face crimson as his mother cuddled him.

'He's been working so hard.'

'Hello, Mrs Benson.'

'Don't call me that. What is it with these private school boys? It isn't the 1950s.'

'I like it,' said Anne. 'I would hate to think that good manners could ever go out of fashion. They all call each other by their surnames, stand for others on crowded buses, address their teachers as sir.'

'Even the female teachers?'

'It isn't a laughing matter, Emma. The school has done a wonderful job. Jason topped the school in economics in the trials. He's a prefect. Aren't you, love?'

'He's never gotten into trouble?'

'I've been kept too busy,' answered Jason, before his mother could extol his virtues further. He was slowly dying inside.

'And who will you take to the School Formal?' asked Emma. 'Or don't you think about such things?'

'He wants to take that young girl from Mosman High who lives near here.'

'Jess?'

'Yes. But I don't think she would feel comfortable going. The other boys are asking Loreto and Monte girls,' said his mother.

'I haven't asked anybody. I don't think I'll even go.'

'You have to go,' said his mother, stepping away and looking him up and down. 'Won't he look handsome in a tuxedo?'

'Yes, you have to go. If only for the tuxedo,' said Emma, smirking.

'You've got half an hour before dinner. Do half an hour more study for me and then you can come out and join us. OK?'

Jason looked from Emma to his mum and back and, even though being treated as a child was boiling his blood, decided that it wasn't such a bad idea. He had suffered enough at the hands of his mother's love and thought only of escape. He did as he was told.

'Can I help with anything?' asked Emma, now she was alone with Anne.

'Umm . . . No, I think I'm fine. The boys are probably playing pool. Can you see if they're alright for drinks?'

Having escaped Anne, Emma was not going to go join her husband and Simon's discussion of the rugby, which was about the only thing the two men had in common. She took a left when she entered the hallway, heading off in search of Jason.

∞

Jason swivelled in his seat when a shadow let him know someone was standing at his door. He knew it was going to be Emma. The hairs on the back of his neck had risen. When he saw the look in her eye, his body shook. She leaned against the door frame. He was unused to these pregnant silences. They shared a secret, a great and dangerous one. It was everywhere between them.

She frightened him, too. She held him in her grip. She could cause so much trouble for him. He watched as she examined his room. He was ashamed of the boyhood treasures which lined every shelf, hung on the walls, lay about in untidy piles in the corners of the room.

To Emma it seemed the room of a much younger man. It was as though the last few years had not passed. What had he been doing? There were no photos of friends, the books on his shelves reflected his twelve-year-old tastes, and the posters she hoped were his mother's doing. What of the man sitting on the child's desk chair? If she was to examine his computer would she find porn? Did he have four hundred Facebook friends? What art did he like? What books? Did he have a thing for foreign films? His room gave her nothing. Nothing but a blank canvas.

'Where were you this afternoon?'

'Mum met me outside school. She gave me a talking to about how much time I have left till my exams and sat down with me to work out this study plan.' He held up a sheet of paper. 'There is not an hour of my life between now and then that isn't taken into account.'

'Do you always do as your parents ask?'

'No.'

'I think you do. And that's OK. I suppose. They want the best for you.'

Jason said nothing.

'You know, if I had seen this room before I . . .'

Jason glanced around.

'I am not my room. I haven't had time to do anything here but study and sleep. They expect so much from me. Do you know I'm in the chess club? I swim, play cricket, tennis and rugby. I'm in the debating team. Until recently I played bass in the school band. I haven't had time to do *anything*.

Why do you think I sometimes wag school? Some days I'm ready to scream. And then I jumped over our fence and found you. Do you know how hard it is to keep going now that all I think about is you?'

'But you have to keep it all going.'

'Why do I?'

Emma walked across to him and kissed his lips.

'Because I'm not real.'

She left the room.

NINE

At dinner Emma seated herself next to Jason. They were at the table in the kitchen, which was the table the family most often used; Emma and David, as neighbours, being considered part of the family. The table was not large and part of the fun was squeezing everybody in. Emma made sure that her hip rested against Jason's hip, that her arm brushed against his as she cut up her food, that her shoulder met his as often as she could manage.

After the meal the conversation turned to politics and Emma found she was unable to join in.

Not because she knew nothing about politics, but because she knew a lot about politics. Simon and Anne were lovely people but if David hadn't struck up a friendship with Simon, Emma wouldn't have had anything to do with them. She bit her tongue for David and turned her attention elsewhere.

Jason had been listening to his father and had been watching the side of Emma's face, seeing it cloud over.

David was being conciliatory. Then Anne joined in and her views made her husband's seem moderate. David forced a laugh but the mood was deteriorating by the second.

'So, Jason, what do you think you'll do next year?' asked David, changing the subject completely, knowing that Simon and Anne loved nothing more than talking about their son. 'Will you take a year off and see the world or leap straight into work?'

'Jason will be going to university,' answered his father. 'Won't you?'

At this moment, something happened to distract Jason. Emma's hand was suddenly in his lap. And before he could speak it was no longer just in his lap but moving up and over his crotch which moved under her.

'Ummm . . . Yes, that's right. University,' he said, trying hard to modulate his voice. Preventing himself from blushing, however, was impossible. He reddened as Emma's hand squeezed him lightly.

The jeans were being stretched tight. She could feel the thing pressing against her. She traced the shape with her fingertips.

'I would have thought you would take a year off. Your mother says you've been working very hard,' said Emma, squeezing his crotch on the final word.

'I'd rather get it all over and done with now,' he said.

Emma could feel his cock straining for release. She wanted to release it, to hold its thickness in her hand. She began unbuttoning his jeans. It was difficult to do one-handed, the material was tight, the buttons fixed against the twitching shaft.

'When I was your age I couldn't wait to get to work but my father convinced me to go to university,' said David. 'I won't say the time was wasted, but some of my peers had made millions while I was at uni.'

'Jason will go straight on. He's quite eager to, aren't you?' said Anne.

Emma had managed to get Jason's fly undone

and had pushed her hand through. She gripped his hard cock through his boxer shorts and pulled it out of his jeans. She was not happy yet. It was still caught in his boxer shorts. She wanted the hot flesh in her hand.

'I bet he's very eager,' said Emma. 'But I think I benefited from taking a year off. I went to Europe and North Africa, saw a bit of the world before I came back here and landed myself a millionaire.'

David laughed at this. He knew that Emma was being mischievous. He just didn't know how mischievous.

She had trouble disentangling Jason's cock from his boxers so she gripped it clothed and started to move her wrist ever so slightly up and down.

Jason leant forward over his food.

'Sit up, Jason,' demanded his mother.

'I went to Sydney University,' said David.

'We met at UNSW,' said Simon, motioning towards Anne.

'I want to go to Canberra,' said Jason.

'Canberra!' cried his parents in unison.

Emma made use of the disturbance to give Jason a more vigorous tug. She knew it wouldn't take long. It was lucky he was still covered up. He lurched forward again.

'You can't go to Canberra,' said his mother.

'Why Canberra, for God's sake?'

Emma knew why and kept on pulling him. She could feel his cock throbbing. She knew what it meant and dearly wanted to make him blow at his parents' table.

'I like the idea of dorm life,' he said, before leaning forward, covering what looked like a spasm with a cough.

'Well, we'll talk about that. Now be a good boy and get your mother a bottle of San Pellegrino from the fridge.'

'Ummm . . .'

Emma stopped her ministrations. The boy's fly was open, his cock stood erect on the edge of orgasm. He could not move. She was in two minds. She wanted to burst out laughing. The boy couldn't do as his mother asked.

Couldn't, not wouldn't.

Couldn't.

He was paralysed. But then she really didn't want her marriage to come to a sudden end tonight either, so she stood up.

'I'll get it.'

∞

Later that night, when David had stepped into the shower, Emma stole out of the house and ran down the side passage between the two houses and crept into Jason's backyard. He was still up watching TV in the rumpus room. Making sure the room was empty she tapped on the glass door. Jason swung round quickly. She could tell she had frightened him.

She motioned for him to come to her and then stepped out of sight.

Jason found her in the side passage. She led him by the hand till they were lost in shadows.

'I so wanted you to come to me this afternoon,' she said. 'Those fucking Speedos.'

'I wanted to be there. I couldn't follow Mum's study plan. She kept tapping me to keep me focused.'

Emma grabbed him and kissed him deeply. She hugged him to her. He fell back against the wall with Emma pushing herself onto him. She rubbed his cock in his jeans.

'Wait. I have to get back. You'd better come over tomorrow. I'll be waiting for you. I have to have you.'

'I'll come.'

'What if your mum says no?'

'Nothing will stop me.'

Then she was gone.

TEN

Jason climbed the fence and, finding Emma's backyard empty, entered the house cautiously. He was too afraid to call out for Emma just in case David was home, yet his fears were not great enough to keep him out.

The back door was open. Emma's towel hung over the kitchen stool. There was the bottle of 30+. This was normal. Emma had been here recently. Besides, she had told him to come over after school. It was after school. If he had kept to his mother's study plan he would be in his room revising Modern History. But he was not keeping to her plan. Emma had set a new schedule for him. And all was as it should be, except for the fact that Emma was not waiting for him in the backyard.

He stood still and listened. The house was completely silent. But it was a big house. She could be waiting for him in her bedroom. The thought gave him courage.

∞

Emma was in the shower. She had been out in the sun but had dozed off while reading and had woken in the shade. Chilled to the bone she had wanted to run a bath for herself but seeing the time and realising Jason could turn up at any moment decided to take a quick hot shower instead. She chose the main bathroom. It was closer to the stairs, giving her a chance of hearing Jason should he call out. Besides, she loved the oversized shower-head in the main bathroom. It was like standing under a waterfall.

Stripping off and stepping inside the shower Emma felt enlivened by expectation. Her lover could appear at any moment. Her young lover. A young man who confessed that he thought only of her.

She began thinking about Jason coming in and finding her showering. If he found her completely naked, what would that mean for him? She had hoped to take things slow. But under the warm stream of the shower she now knew it would be more difficult than she previously supposed.

She began thinking about Jason's cock. She hadn't seen it yet but had held its heavy form through his boxer shorts which were so thin she could feel the veins and the ridges through them. While she had been playing with Jason all she could think about was having the thing in her mouth. She'd have crawled under the table if the world would have permitted her.

Emma had always loved sucking a man's cock. She felt it was the only way to *really* make a man come. When she had a cock in her mouth, when she gripped the base with her hand, when she teased the underside of the shaft with her tongue she knew that she was able to make her man scream, faint, growl, beg, demand; she knew that everything he was feeling was under her control. The orgasm she would extract, after much teasing, was inevitably one which would be more intense and more overwhelming than any he had caused by his own hand or had extracted through fucking.

She showered thinking of Jason. She recalled his face as he came. She would make his first blow job give him white hair. She wanted to make him wait. To hear him stifle his screams, to have him grab her hair in his passion only to release it in his fear of hurting her. She would lay her head on his thigh and slowly suck and tease while she played with herself. Again she would hide from him that she was experiencing orgasm. She wanted to have his breath shorten and wanted his hips to buck as he tried to fuck her mouth. But every time he'd buck she'd stop and blow lightly on his cock.

She thought about this while under the hot steady stream of her shower, every moment expecting to hear the sound of Jason approaching. She felt very vulnerable. She began to think of the shower door being pulled open and a man other than Jason appearing there. She felt her heart stop just at the thought.

Then she imagined David coming home and finding her in the shower with Jason. She thought of what David would do if she were on her knees and sucking Jason under the hot stream.

Turned on by all these daydreams she ran her hand down her body, twisting the stream towards the wall. She leant her whole body against the wall and slipped her fingers between her legs with the water running over her head and face and down her back.

She fantasised about David coming in and finding her like this. He loved to watch her or to catch her doing it. She played with herself and imagined David in full fury. She imagined him discovering her with Paul, the only man she had been with since her wedding, his good friend. She pictured David's face. She had witnessed it distorted with anger but never yet directed at her. David was a powerful presence when angry. She imagined him catching her out, standing in the bathroom immobilised by rage. She would be terrified at the sight. Fearful of the harm he might do to Paul, or Jason, or her.

And then she'd think of David fucking her while he was angry. She could feel his thrusts like punches into her. Emma could feel his cock in her, she felt his breath against her neck. She thought of Jason's cock spurting out come as she thought of David's cock pounding into her. She felt her orgasm wash over her in two slow waves of pleasure.

Emma lay against the wall and smiled while continuing to play with herself. Her lust knew no bounds, and when she began thinking of Jason coming in whilst she was gasping the little breaths of orgasm, she began to feel the second orgasm waiting in line impatiently, so before the first was properly savoured Emma was heading for the second. She imagined Jason waiting shyly at the door whilst he listened to her coming in the shower. She imagined him imagining her sucking his cock while he pulled away at it listening to her moaning while she fingered herself in the shower.

Emma was incredibly aroused. Her body was jumping in spasms which drove her against the wall and against her hand and fingers. She even began thrusting into her hand. She wanted so much to see his young face during orgasm, like on that first day. She wanted him. Fuck! she wanted him.

She felt her climax, dodged it, jumped on it and embraced it. She came again, violently, she screamed out, Fuck! She felt so fucking horny, so fucking there. As the orgasm left her she only wanted more. She slowed down and let the water run over her. She wanted to be held, to be kissed and kissed. She wanted to eat a man and was glad that Jason would come soon if her scream hadn't frightened him off. He might have thought she was with David.

She lay against the tiles letting the wall take most of her weight. She felt young and fresh and sexy and beautiful. She wanted to give herself to every man and woman. The way she felt was not new to her, she often felt like giving herself to others. She loved the freedom she had. Her body was her own to give and she wanted to give it to everyone. She received such pleasure from the mere thought of giving pleasure to others.

Mmmm, she murmured, feeling the reverberations run through her. She loved to be fucked, touched, adored, held, scratched, kissed and caressed. She glanced across her past and imagined a room of her lovers coming back to fuck her all over again.

ELEVEN

The shower started to lose its warmth, which annoyed Emma not a little. It altered her mood and she decided to get out. She had hoped Jason would come and find her in the shower but he hadn't and now the water was getting cold. She opened the shower door, reached out for her towel and closed the door again before all the hot air escaped. She towelled herself down, her buoyant mood deflating. Jason hadn't kept his promise.

'Emma?' came a squeal from the door, quickly followed by 'Emma?' in a deeper voice. She jumped, startled away from her glum thoughts. She wrapped the towel around herself and slowly opened the screen door.

Emma saw Jason through the mist. He stood at the door, nervous like a deer. If she made one wrong move she feared he would be off down the hall in a flash.

She stepped out onto the bath mat smiling at him and watching his eyes take her body in.

'I love the way you look at me, Jason.'

'You are beautiful,' he said.

'Thank you. So are you.'

Jason frowned, his petulant youthful nature coming through once again.

'Do you like what you see?' she asked, thinking it banal as she did so and wishing she could come up with better things to say.

'I love you,' he said.

'Then give me a kiss.'

Jason's large body ambled forward and he leant his face to hers. She turned from his kiss.

'Not there,' she said, as he lifted his face to look at her. 'Here.' She raised her foot slightly. She had to curb her actions again. She forgot he had yet to see her naked. She put her foot on the edge of the bath and pushed the towel between her legs so he couldn't steal a peek; especially as it was then, wet and hot and thoroughly debauched.

With one hand holding the towel to her breast and the other against the glass of the shower door Emma was unable to touch her young lover. She wanted to touch him – to take off his t-shirt for one thing. He bent over obediently and gave her foot an uninspiring kiss.

'That is the way you kiss your grandmother.'

'What?'

'That's my foot. Not your grandmother's face. My foot wants you, Jason. Kiss it properly.'

He knelt down. He placed his lips on the smooth clean skin. Then he thought about what it was he was kissing. Emma's foot. He looked up at her and she looked down at him calmly. He placed little kisses along her foot and brought his lips against her toes. The bright idea of using his tongue entered his head. He kissed her toes gently with his lips parted, tasting her skin.

She tasted so fresh. There were droplets of water on her foot, which heightened his appreciation in this moment. He fleetingly compared her soft white skin with what he considered his most favourite expression of freshness. An apple from the fridge in summer. Washed under the tap and dripping. He would love the anticipation of the freshness as much as the actual attainment of the crisp cold apple itself.

He thought of this as we all tend to think; the idea coming and going unexamined, leaving him with an undefined hunger. He thought of biting and eating her. His cock hardened and pulsed. His tongue darted out between her toes and she giggled. Then he thought to draw a toe into his mouth.

He moved his body, and sat down on the cool tiled floor with his back against the side of the bath. He held her foot and rested the soft flesh of the ball of her foot against his chin. He looked up at her. She pushed the towel down between her legs, but he wasn't even thinking of that. He wanted to know if anyone had ever thought of doing this. He took her tiny toe into his mouth. He swirled his tongue around it and sucked on it. He visualised his tongue sucking her skin. He massaged her calf with one hand and kneaded her heel with the other. He then moved onto the next toe.

His erection was urging him all the while. The pressure it was exerting was substantial. Foreplay was not on his cock's agenda for the day. In fact, it never would be. There was a slow chant. Come, Come, Come. An insistent and persuasive message which men heeded all too often. But Jason continued to suck on her toes, and took great pleasure in it. He wanted to please. He needed to please. He wanted Emma to be feeling as he felt and more. The chant in his pants continued but obviously Emma's influence was greater.

'That's what I wanted. A proper kiss,' she said, thinking immediately of his hot, inexperienced kisses making their way up her body. She wondered where to take him. The bedroom?

Then he rubbed his hand along the underside of her leg and under the towel. A moment of alarm became a moment of exhilaration as she thought of him breaking her rules and touching her. Even the thought of reprimanding him thrilled her. She let his warm rough hand run and run. She wanted him to touch her. She needed his fingers to penetrate her. She felt so warm and so wet. She wanted to know what he would do. How he would cope with a pussy bursting with desire.

But he baulked. His hand stopped and then cautiously slipped around and caressed and then gripped her butt. She was balancing on one leg with her other raised while he sucked her toes one by one. She could hardly concentrate. The simple pleasure of his warm mouth against her toes was sending shivers through her and the knowledge that his hand was on her butt insisted on a quick end to her games. His hand was pulling her to him and she was resting her weight against it in reply.

She was reminded of lovers who had taken her in their hands. Lovers who had lifted her, moved her, shifted her and mounted her. She loved to be within the hands of a lover, to have their hands grabbing her butt while they fucked her with all their might. Her desires were well fuelled. Her memories matched her imaginative powers. Every thought rolled in with footnotes and further examples. Her lust snowballed quickly.

'Take off your top!' she said. 'Oh fuck! Let's go!'

'Where?' he asked, looking up at her from the floor.

He took in her whole body and yearned for her. He wanted to taste every part of her, to lick her skin. Lick it. Lick it all.

He thought a new thought. Something he had never connected with his own experience. He remembered a photo a boy had shown him years and years ago. It was a picture of a woman licking another woman's vagina. He must have been ten when he saw it. This was the image that came to him when he thought of Emma's skin. When he desired her skin and wanted to lick it and taste it with his mouth. His mouth was hungry for her. He thought of the photo and wanted to kiss Emma like that.

Emma steadied herself, placing both of her feet onto the tiles, clutching the towel which really wanted to be a pile on the floor – or was that Emma's wish? She thought it time to stand naked in front of him. To reveal all. Did she? Damn these games. Emma looked down at her boy. His blue jeans were ragged at the ends. He wore no shoes. She liked that about him. His brown feet and ankles looked edible coming from that deep ocean blue. They always looked clean too. She liked her own feet and she liked feet. Jason's would go well with a bit of melon.

He had on a nasty blue sport t-shirt with the school's name printed on the left breast. But it was tight in the right places and it brought the age difference into focus which excited Emma. She was a schoolboy's lover.

'What's that?' she asked, in a sweet voice, pointing at his crotch. His cock was pressing

painfully against his tight jeans. She smiled at
him, a smile which acknowledged the childish nature of her question. She knew that her
question was one she had asked him before but
repetition seldom dulled her sexual fantasies.
Repetition was one of the champions of pleasure. All of her thoughts were slight variations
of themes she had cherished during her sexual
life. She dearly wanted to kneel down there and
investigate, to release his straining cock. In fact,
a passing thought ran through her mind of being
butt fucked by Jason whilst she sucked Jason's
cock for the first time. A stupid thought but a
highly arousing one. To have two Jasons, the
Jason she would soon have and the Jason she had
now, loving her at the same time.

'Nothing,' he said.

'Doesn't look like nothing. Let me see.' Saying this she knelt down, clutching the towel to
her front, and leant forward. Jason's eyes found
uncovered places. Emma knelt and brought her
face right up close to his crotch. She was silent. Her
wet hair dangled around her face. She studied the
stitches and then the form behind them. She had
fondled it through lighter material than denim.
She wondered what she'd do. She wondered . . .

She found his seriousness contagious. Her every movement was meaningful for Jason. Each touch was registered, each lesson memorised.

She was a ball now, her forehead resting against his crotch. She could feel it jump and spasm under her. She was worried. All the forces in her body were screaming out. She wanted to finish the games. She no longer wished to be a teacher.

He began to smooth her wet hair. The innocence of this act was lost on Emma. She had felt that hand a million times. The hand which urged her to suck, urged her to take it all the way in; that hand which stopped her play and demanded strong sucking and quick rhythm. Jason's touch was soft but gave her no direction. Emma was confused. At this point a firm hand would change everything. Would she break? She would, she would, she answered nodding her head slowly, rubbing herself against him.

'Yes,' she thought. 'Yes.'

Jason had been still all the while. His balls were beginning to ache. Every day now he had a pain there, a pain which was only dulled by masturbating. Every time he left Emma he had had to run home to jerk off. Sometimes three or four times in a row, quickly and eagerly. He would lock himself in the bathroom and then, staring in the mirror, would pull himself to a quick climax whilst thinking of her.

Sometimes he would even say her name. Sometimes he would curse her. Sometimes he would whisper obscenities. 'Suck it, bitch! Suck it!' he'd whisper while pulling away. He would shake all over and his butt would clench and he would think physical thoughts, of bodies jamming against each other, of strong hugs and sometimes he thought of hurting, of punching, of wrestling.

He would feel such a great wave of relief when the come shot out, hot drops would spurt into the sink and stick to the dry porcelain. If it touched his hand it was warm and sticky.

He wanted so much in these moments of coming. Many of his desires were blind urges. But some were clear. He wanted to fuck Emma. *That* was clear. It wasn't so clear when it came to particulars. He couldn't visualise penetration, or what it would feel like. He wanted so badly to know. Sometimes while showering he would soap up his hand and make a fist and then shove his hard-on into it. He would pretend his fist was Emma. One afternoon she had asked him how he masturbated and Jason had told her he didn't do it often. He told her that he would do it in bed under the covers and that it wasn't very good. She hadn't believed him. She knew boys in their teens were obsessive masturbators. She knew many girls were too. She had been.

Emma restrained herself. She rubbed her head against the bulge in his jeans but then pulled away. Just a little.

'I want to suck it, Jason,' she said quietly. She didn't look up but kept her eyes fixed on his crotch. She thought she knew what these words would mean to him. She was turned on further by the very idea of his supposed thoughts. But she was also contemplative, concerned with her own heavy need to have his body.

Jason failed to speak. A confusing array of images and sensations rushed his mind. Fear was a factor in his being struck dumb. He was so often burnt, both by Emma's playful teasing and by the failure of any of his reasonable boyish expectations being realised, that he immediately assumed that this new, spoken desire of Emma's was just another in a long line of disappointments. But young men live on hope and evidence is often ignored in favour of less likely, and less plausible, possibilities. That she would suck his cock! That she would finally break through and touch him as he had always hoped she would!

On the one hand it was the most obvious end to their fooling around. But on the other, on the hand that Emma always held out of reach, there sat a fat god called reality. This god, this option number two, reminded him of his pimples, of his voice cracking, of the simple fact that he was completely out of his depth.

'Show me it,' said Emma. She had not moved. Somehow moving would be an indication that she was coming to her senses. If she remained utterly still, if she felt the cold tiles against her shins, if she could feel the warmth between her legs she was okay. Her words could be spoken without consequences. She did so want to see his cock. But she knew. She knew about . . . She knew damn well that she was teasing herself and her boy. She knew it.

'Show me it, Jason. I want to see it.'

Jason was able to look at her while she concentrated on his crotch. She was staring so intently. She was rolled up and small and childlike. He was surprised at the level of her fascination and he saw the humour in it. He managed that much. But he was frightened by her intensity. Her behaviour did appear a kind of madness. She wants to see my cock, he was thinking. Suck it! was the chant that echoed in the background of every thought which passed through his mind. Suck it!

'Show me it!' she said again. She looked up, lifting her head slightly. Her control had dispersed. And the moment changed the direction in which everything was heading.

'No.'

The spell broke.

TWELVE

Emma sat up, her towel was left on her lap and her breasts were unceremoniously revealed to her young lover. His eyes were full of them. He had been waiting for this moment. He had caught glimpses of her breasts, he had seen how they fell braless in her tight tops, how they hung in her bikini as she lay on her stomach and rested on her elbows. He had ogled them long before he had ever thought of Emma as anything but the pretty lady next door. Now they were naked and within reach. Large, soft breasts, wonderful breasts, he stared and instinctively his hand reached up and his index finger traced the curve of her right breast. It was as if a charge had issued from them. His hand conducted a power which ignited his mind and cock.

Emma looked on at first embarrassed, then startled and then pleased and excited. His sweet reverence cancelled any of her misgivings. She had pictured the moment differently, but this was turning out to be more beautiful than she had planned. Before her eyes, in a matter of seconds, his youthful wonder was merging directly into a mature desire – it was magic.

Jason glanced up at her – his eyes conveying to her his need for her to trust him. She looked at him like a lover, a new lover, but not necessarily a young lover. She nodded the slightest of nods. He felt no change in her. He had no time for thought. He brought his other hand near her nipple. He had scrambled up now so that he was on his knees. Her face was clear of the madness of a few moments ago. She had taken on a new role. And was drinking in his enthusiasm.

He felt his body tense and his mouth watered. He paused for a moment, suddenly aware of where he was and this brought new enthusiasm to the situation.

Just for a split second he stepped back mentally, like a director considering his scene. Jason's scene was Emma's breasts. He already heard himself, years from now, telling the tale of the next-door neighbour whose breasts he touched. Jason was proud and felt powerful because of it.

He leant forward and watched closely as his hand touched her nipple, just brushing the skin. He was cautious. Her breasts wanted so much from him but he only knew what instinct told him, he knew of biting and sucking, he wanted them whole. But he sensed some code. He also knew that he had to behave in a way which suited Emma's feelings. After all they were her breasts even though their sudden exposure had narrowed his vision and his appreciation of the wider world. His focus was intense.

'You're breaking my rules,' said Emma in a husky voice. She held her breath as his finger circled her nipple, then released it when he moved his finger away.

'You're so . . .' he said, not able to finish as he brought his mouth close to her nipple.

She felt his breath. He saw the tiny blonde hairs and the pores in her skin, he saw the rosy tint of her aureole appear out of the milky soft flesh.

Both nipples were erect and for a moment there was not a sound, not a breath, as his mouth came to rest softly against her breast, his lips making an 'o' around her nipple.

Heat. He flicked his tongue against her nipple, barely touching it. Then she moaned. It was unlike many of Emma's moans – this one had no prelude. It escaped as naturally as a scream from a fright.

This moan excited her devious mind. But it also surprised her. The shudder of pleasure that seemed to sound an end rather than a beginning was unqualified and intense.

The mental pleasure of her seduction had been revealed as a far deeper physical one. This excited her more. Never before had she felt so like her lover. She was beginning to feel the excitement she assumed Jason was experiencing, one that she had failed to experience in her mad rush to experience every pleasure she could. She had never taken her time. Gimme, gimme, gimme . . . had been her motto. She had never been a boy. She had never been a girl. She had despised normal boys and normal girls. They were complacent and sated. Small pleasures amused them and, to her general dismay, they appeared satisfied with the slow speed of their development. And she still thought that she was right to despise them. She *half* thought she was right to. The older she got the more she wanted. She wanted more for the Emma of the past and the Emma of the future. Lately she had begun to want to have been the parallel Emma, the Emma who didn't move at breakneck speed through adolescence. Now she really wanted to experience life timidly. It was something which she had thought was outside the realm of her experience, until now. Now she felt this beautiful new appreciation. This moment with Jason was lived vicariously. His awe was the key. He was living each moment fully aware of the movements of his lover, drawing meaning from them and making judgements from them. He had placed his trust in Emma, knowing and accepting that at times she would betray it or at the very least toy with it, and he relied on her dominance completely.

That moan had signalled an end of the pretence that she was in control. She had been swallowed whole by her own fantasy and had emerged a part of it. Layers of manipulative planning ceased to exist in one sudden burst of simple pleasure.

Again his mouth teased her nipple and again she was faced with the sweet pleasures of celebrated inexperience. So many men and women had done just what was being done now and yet . . . Nothing like it had been done.

She had kissed more with Jason than she had done for years. Being kissed. Kissing. Jason wanted to kiss her, he wanted never to have to stop kissing her. The teacher was being taught. Each touch of the tongue, each breath and movement was pleasurable and exciting. But these excitements led nowhere. This was the lesson that Emma had had to learn. Kissing was the end in itself. Jason had been more than happy with her kisses. So Jason had altered her as surely as she was altering him. But he did so unnoticed. What she hadn't counted on and what was most welcome and surprising was the change in her.

Jason's breathing was getting faster, he was shaking with the blind and unacknowledged frustration that this unexpected feast was inducing. Running through him was mad desire, an adult lust that he did not know how to act upon. He felt excited and hungry. He felt what his eyes and mouth saw and tasted. He had anticipated a reaction and was rewarded with Emma's moan. He was fully functional. He could roar like a wild beast. But he shook and his hands, which he raised to touch her hips and stomach, were weak. He wanted to lie her down and climb onto her. But he was fearful. He wanted to do things he didn't know about, or was unsure about. He knew what a man did to a woman when they had sex. He'd seen enough porn. What he didn't know was how he, Jason, could do it. Every part of him was surging. He was hard and his balls ached. Her breasts, like a red rag to a bull, were determining his entire world.

He took a deep breath.

'Baby!' whispered Emma. 'What's the matter?'

'Do you like it?' he asked, staring up at her.

'Do you want the truth?'

He nodded.

'I'm in a dream world. Kiss them. Kiss them more,' she whispered, looking at him and, for that moment, loving him. She had played so many games, had been so many people and so many Emmas that this time, when she really wanted to convey to her lover the truth, she doubted her ability to. She heard the words and knew their truth but worried nonetheless.

She needn't have, Jason's critical faculty was not even switched on, these words filled him to the brim. He leaped forward, not in space but in confidence. Jason looked from her face to her breasts and took one in each hand. Emma's hands joined his, she placed hers on the back of his and directed and was led as together they caressed her breasts.

Emma was drifting in and out of that curious new state. She tried to keep herself in it, she tried to remain the new lover, but Jason was behaving differently. He kissed her breast and then bit her nipple. A kind of madness had crept up on him. He saw and hungered for her breasts and felt that Emma had given him permission to do as he pleased. He assumed that he was being a good and impassioned lover. He squeezed her nipple.

'Gently,' she whispered. She had let him go for a bit, she was half enjoying the artlessness of his attack, but that bite had hurt and his movements were becoming faster and harder. He took her nipple into his mouth while rubbing and squeezing her breast and his hunger directed him to bite again.

'Hey, that hurt!' she said, pushing him away. 'Don't do that!'

Jason stared at her, uncomprehending. She saw that he was stupefied. She was a little amazed at her own behaviour. There had been lovers before who had been rough and there would be rough lovers to come. But somehow Jason wasn't allowed to be that way. His roughness should have been a turn on – wasn't it why she was with a young, inexperienced lover? It might have been. But things change. Emma was changing. The situation wasn't as it had been.

When she had masturbated while showering she had thought of Jason as something of a plaything. She had plotted and schemed. But now she wanted to share the experiences of young love. She wanted Jason to love her as though she were eighteen too – to be cautious and fearful and careful. She knew that Jason was reacting to Emma the older woman, the woman who was experienced and who had seduced him. She suddenly wanted to cry. She was confused and seeing Jason's young face staring at her like that made her feel awful. She felt the consequences of her behaviour rolling towards her like a freak wave. To dabble so casually in something as important as someone's adolescence! To take pleasure in another's inexperience. Men have done it. She had been the willing recipient of a number of men's efforts to educate her, to lead her, mould her. Wasn't Jason reaching out to her? Wasn't he a willing participant too? She doubted this. She knew how to manipulate men. She found it easy. It was easy. Jason was eighteen.

'Are you OK?' he asked, after an awkward few moments.

'I'm fine. I just thought you were getting a bit rough. I'm sorry I pushed you away. You've made me a bit crazy today. You're just too damn cute and I am too damn . . .' She leant forward and placed her palm against his cheek and then kissed him. He left the kiss.

'What?' he asked.

'I give in to my desires too easily. No, that isn't right. I place my desires before . . . Yes that's it.'

'What?'

'Am I a bad person?'

'No.'

'Good,' she said. 'Kiss me again.'

He kissed her, and kept his hands by his side. Her kiss was possessive. He understood that she still liked him. He was warmed and relieved by this kiss. But he was also still bursting at the seams. If she had decided then and there to undo his jeans she would have caused him to come by the mere presence of her hand. His balls ached and his hard-on demanded release. He still wanted to eat her. He would have carved her up and eaten her

THE SECRET LIVES OF EMMA

raw and he would have been sated. Yes, to have her! That was the theme of his new novel, possession. He wanted to have her. He didn't know how. But he wanted it now.

'I don't know what I'm going to do with you. You make me crazy,' she said, and she brought him close and hugged him. He was very aware that her naked breasts were pressed against him but he restrained himself from acting upon the many impetuous directives his cock was sending him.

'Well?' she asked after a while.

'I don't know,' he said.

'I think you should go,' she said. 'No. That sounded bad. Don't worry. We went a bit far. But I want to have my cake and eat it too. I'm sorry. I should have stopped. But when I saw your face I felt so, mmm, and then you touched my nipple and . . . you know.' She made to laugh and then just sighed. 'You're so damn cute, Jason. I should have more restraint. You're young, you have much to learn and I have much to teach. I had plans for you, Jason. I was going to teach you everything.' She turned his head so that she could plant little kisses on his lips. 'And you're a good kisser and you're beautiful and I want to do things to you.'

She kissed him properly. He was eager and she held him tightly.

'Now go and leave me in peace. I'm a mess.'

Jason left with barely a word. She heard him go down the stairs. But then she thought of something. She ran to the stairs leaving the towel behind. She called after him. He turned from the back door and came to the bottom of the stairs. She hid behind the corner and looked down on him. He gazed up at her smiling.

'Don't you rush off home and pull off. I want you to promise me you won't,' she said.

Jason's face reddened.

'Come on, I know you were. Why else would you leave a half-naked slut like me so fast, with barely a goodbye?'

She observed his face with amusement; he was actually shocked by her words.

'Promise me you won't,' she repeated.

'I wasn't going to,' he said. 'You're crazy, Emma.'

'Don't do it! Go home now. But be good!'

THIRTEEN

Emma was making dinner for David and herself, but nothing was going quite to plan. She couldn't keep her mind on the task at hand and she kept stopping mid-action. Her mind was filled with thoughts of Jason.

David was late and dinner was turning into an unmitigated disaster. Frustrated with her efforts she abandoned the attempt and glanced out the kitchen window across the side passage towards the blackened window of Simon and Anne's large rumpus room. As she did so someone switched the light on. She moved back from her window and picked up the abandoned mushrooms and started chopping them. But she knew that if you stood in the right spot, her kitchen window afforded a fairly good view of the rumpus room. This knowledge would not let her be. She had to know if Jason had turned on the light. She wanted to look at him. To talk with him. She needed to see him.

She turned off the light and leaned over the counter to peer across the way. Jason was sitting on the couch with the phone to his ear. He was facing away from her. The TV was on. Emma wanted desperately to go over to him but she expected David home at any moment. She hadn't rung Jason before for fear of alerting his parents to their mismatch of a friendship. But she took a chance, counting on them to have Call Waiting.

Jason answered.

'I can see you, cutie,' she said, and watched him turn around and look in her direction.

'I can't see you,' he said, and she saw him trying to.

'Good,' she answered. 'Who are you speaking to?'

'Jess.'

Emma felt a pang of jealousy and then laughed at herself.

'Your girlfriend?' she teased.

'No . . . no.'

'Doesn't matter. I want you to come here at . . . um . . . come at twelve. I'll leave the back door open.'

'I can't, Emma.'

'Why can't you? Are you meeting Jess?'

'No. I can't get out of here. Mum and Dad will hear.'

'Can't you move quietly? I want you here at twelve,' she demanded. 'I need you,' she added.

'I'll try.'

'You better come, or I'll come and find you.'

'OK, OK.'

'Bye.'

'Bye.'

She hung up and then she smiled mischievously and dialled again.

'Hello?'

'Did you pull off?'

'No,' he said.

'Did you want to?'

There was a pause. She listened to his breathing.

'Tell me. Jess is waiting,' she urged.

'Yes,' he sighed.

'Can you hold on till tonight?'

'Yes.'

'OK, bye.'

'Bye.'

'Wait! Jason, are you there?'

'Yeah.'

'I didn't wait,' she revealed and hung up.

Jason was lying in his bed in his parents' house. He was dozing. Dreams seduced him from consciousness. In his hand he held his alarm clock. His finger was still on the button to silence it when it went off. Now he slept. It was ten-thirty, the alarm was set for twelve.

In his dreams he overslept his appointed time. He slept badly and tossed and turned, rolling onto the alarm clock as he did so. Now his dreams were made worse by the uncomfortable presence of the small square of plastic and metal beneath his lower back. He dreamt of being stabbed. He woke up.

Seeing nothing in the dark room he reached up to switch on the light. He felt the pain of the lost clock in his back and he pulled it out and looked at it. He still had an hour or so to wait. He turned off the light and clutched the clock to him. He felt aroused. His cock was rigid in his pyjamas. No dreamed stabbing could calm his body tonight. He was anxious and edgy. Since that day he jumped over Emma's fence he seemed to spend his life on edge. She made him so hot.

He was constantly thinking about her. The way she talked to him, the way she touched him, the way she let him touch her and how she looked and felt.

He was full of her.

He couldn't concentrate at school.

He couldn't concentrate at home.

He was beginning to realise the enormity of what they were doing. His mind was a pendulum of indecision. Everything she said was new. It was as if she saw life from a completely different perspective to his. And he had to admit that he preferred her perspective. He had always been so abrupt in his thinking and she was softening the lines which bound every one of his ideas.

He lay in the darkness thinking about her. He was unable to sleep. His mind had charged his body once again. All it took these days was a single thought. Jason had become obsessed with certain parts of his lover's body. He loved thinking that she was his lover. He thought of her stomach, the lovely shape of her belly. Her feet. Her fingers. Lips. The weight of her against him, her body pressed, jammed against his.

In his bed that night, holding the alarm, he wished the time would tick faster on to twelve. He had an erection and under the bed covers he was stroking his cock. Emma had warned him not to masturbate that night but the thought of her watching him kiss her stomach and the pleasure he was able to give her while kissing her breasts that very afternoon had made his cock throb painfully for release.

He had been thinking of Emma in an entirely different way. Before today he hadn't been in any hurry to see her nude. The few times when they had been together he had loved what she had given him to love. The actual speed of progress taken was in Emma's hands. But this afternoon had changed that. He had moved things along. He had taken her breasts in his hands and she had let him. Now he wanted more.

Since he had left her house he had been thinking of her breasts, he had been thinking of her skin and of her head rubbing up against his cock. He had gone to the bathroom twice to pull off before his mother had come home. He couldn't shake the hard-on. Every thought he had strengthened its resolve to stay about. He couldn't hang around his mother. He put on a longer t-shirt and when he heard her come home he tucked his erection under the elastic of his boxers and tried to think of anything but Emma. His mum didn't notice and he was safe, but the hard-on remained and his balls still ached.

He wasn't thinking very sensibly. His mother asked him if he was worried about anything. He managed another lie and went off to watch TV. On the way he stopped at the bathroom, went in and locked the door. He undid his jeans. He touched the shaft and it jumped. He was staring at himself in the mirror. He knew that two or three strokes would do it. He looked at himself, eyeball to eyeball.

'Do it!' he said. He stroked it once and the pleasure was intense. He felt the orgasm begin. He stopped. He looked at his thick cock, which was longer and harder than it had been before. It throbbed. His was a hard, sensitive cock, bursting to blow. He stroked it again and his left knee wobbled, the orgasm rushed in and then just as quickly receded as he let go.

The pleasure was painful. He moaned and then

buckled himself up and left the bathroom for the safety of the backroom where he turned on the TV. Every once in a while he slyly rubbed his cock through the thin cotton of his jeans pocket.

Saying that he could 'hold on' was one thing. Lying in bed for a few hours drifting in and out of erotic dreams, lying awake with erotic thoughts, well, this was something else altogether. Not reaching climax was his point of honour. But it was sending his mind into curious patterns of thought.

He mused over the changes taking place in him without being critical, which is to say that the thoughts came and went without mental comment. He knew that he felt virile and manly, he knew that he could charge ahead in battle, he knew that he had a beautiful woman waiting for him, he knew the situation was implausible but he also knew he was capable of taking what she offered.

He lay there thinking and feeling all these thoughts and never thinking one of them without another crashing into it, so that not one sensation, not one thought was highlighted or isolated, all were merged and knotted. Power was the over-all effect. He felt, but did not express, this power.

∞

Emma was awake. David had come home in a rotten mood. They had talked for a whole ten minutes in the two hours that he was home before he took himself off to bed. He apologised to her as he went. He said he was being unfair to her but he couldn't shake the mood so it was better to go to sleep and try again tomorrow.

Emma was not an unreasonable person, she knew that sometimes the world was too big, too cruel and too hard, but she also knew that she wasn't all those things to her husband. David could have talked to her. She had tried to draw him out. She had tried to get the lid off his bottled feelings, to at least discover the cause of his mood. But he had shaken off these efforts. He put the TV between Emma and himself. And then he went alone to bed.

Only once David was gone did Emma regret phoning Jason. She found the regret disquieting. She began to wonder whether she had in fact been the cause of her husband's mood. She had been so preoccupied with Jason.

Emma switched off the TV. The room fell silent. She dragged herself from the couch and walked into the kitchen where she found that David had taken the trouble to stack the dishwasher and wipe the benches before he went off to bed. When he had announced that he was going to bed Emma had said 'Goodnight' without looking away from the TV and without searching for a kiss. She, too, was fed up by this stage. A sulky husband is no fun whatsoever.

He had gone and she had continued to watch a depressing documentary on biological warfare. This fits my mood perfectly, she thought. When the documentary ended her life felt a little lighter by comparison. She had seen footage of a dirty fridge in an unsecured lab in Russia which contained enough of a superbug in old jars to wipe out the whole world. Her sulky husband problems now seemed laughable in the face of the total annihilation of life on earth.

Thankfully, for most of us, the great issues of this world are easily shelved while we deal with the smaller issues of our daily existence. Sometimes these weighty issues are completely forgotten moments after they have been reported to us by an earnest and well-meaning journalist simply because the phone rings. Emma found that this sudden exposure to the terrors of Russia's bankrupt biological warfare department had bumped her out of her specific 'My husband's a pig' mood into a general 'The world is an evil place' mood which only has a shelf life of approximately two and a half minutes in the average optimist's mind. If Emma was anything she was an optimist.

So by the time she reached the kitchen and discovered that her husband had cleaned up, which she greedily took as a sign that he at least liked her, her mood had bounced back and she was once again herself. That is, her natural life-loving and thoughtful self who always believed that the pleasures in this life were hers simply because she looked for them in earnest.

Emma began to make herself a cup of tea and glanced at the wall clock to see that it was half past ten. The time had made her feel weary. That same weariness a person might experience when they realise they have to wait an hour for the next bus.

FOURTEEN

Emma sat at the kitchen table with her head resting on her hands. She was asleep. All of the kitchen lights were on so that the room was brilliantly lit. To Jason, standing in the half-light outside the window, the scene was oppressive. Emma's still, silent form in that room of daily productivity made him think of murder, of the unnatural, for she did look unnatural sitting as she was, where she was, at the prearranged time of their rendezvous.

She looked still enough to be dead, though he knew she must be sleeping, but then he was afraid she might be weeping softly. Her hair was in disarray, spread out over the table. He thought of warm, thick blood oozing from a wound to the head, making a puddle. He imagined a thunderous row and a blow to the skull. David had always frightened him. His personality wasn't frightening, it was more his great, physical presence. Jason shrank from him. And yet here he was, peering through the man's window. Emma sanctioned Jason's behaviour. The responsibility was not his. It was Emma's.

His primary fear was of being caught by his parents. His heart beat more regularly now that he had escaped soundlessly from his home. He tapped lightly on the window, so lightly he failed to make a sound. The lit room gave him pause. Could David be up? He had been watching her for at least fifteen minutes. Time hung heavily. But he couldn't open the door, he wouldn't even try the handle to see if it was unlocked.

Quite unexpectedly Emma moved. Jason flinched and ducked. Then he waited a mere moment and raised himself slowly and peeked over the sill. Emma's head was still down but she was wiping her mouth. She lifted herself ever so slowly and proceeded to rub her eyes. Her hair was everywhere. Jason suddenly saw the funny side of her falling asleep. He smiled as he watched Emma come to realise what she had done. She spun around to see the time on the microwave and then her eyes flew to the door. When she turned to the window Jason saw her jump in fright, then smile and beckon him in. Her face had such a muddled, sleepy expression.

Jason made his way to the door and opened it. He now beckoned Emma.

She walked over to him.

'What?' she asked in her normal voice. Jason cringed and raised his forefinger to his lips, the international sign of shush! Emma threw him a very cheeky smile and said in a louder than normal voice, 'Why should I be quiet, Jason? What's the matter?'

The young man had sprung from his position at the door to the safety of the shadows. Now Emma was laughing. She went to the door and called out to him, 'Jason! Jason! Whereforarthoujason?'

Out in the shadows Jason was dying a thousand deaths. Had Emma gone mad? Was this a trap? The delight on her face seemed cruel. Emma could still see him, hiding though he was. He hadn't run home.

'Why do you run from me, Jason?'

'Be quiet, Emma,' he hissed.

'But why? I don't understand. Come and give me a kiss, you young stud. Come inside.'

Jason was sure David was awake now and listening. He almost felt, in the morgue-like silence of suburbia, as though Emma's voice could wake the whole neighbourhood. He was appalled.

Emma was just having a bit of fun at the boy's expense. She was well aware that David would not be woken by noises or voices in the night. She was certain of it. He may wake to go to the loo. He may wake realising she was not asleep beside her, but he wouldn't wake at the sound of her voice or voices. As horrible as having to explain herself to David would be, or worse still, having to explain herself to Jason's parents, the promise of this moment made her willing to take risks. The thrill spoke in a clear simple language her whole body could understand.

But poor Jason hadn't a clue. He was expecting the worst. His knees might have been knocking together out there like some cartoon character. She hoped they were. She wanted him on high alert.

If the truth be known, Emma had little idea of what she was going to do with Jason. That afternoon had been one of the most deliciously frustrating of her entire sexual life. Sending him home, postponing pleasure, denying herself gratification was exciting. But she could not hold out indefinitely. When she had made the call to him she was calling as one sexual adult to another. She wanted for Jason to come over and fulfil the promise of the afternoon. The cup had spilled over and her desire had been unchecked.

But now, her blood having cooled, she was once more in control and saw Jason for what he was, a young, inexperienced lover. He wasn't capable of taking her the way she had wanted. But he *was* capable. That afternoon's play had uncovered much. Emma was surprised by her feelings for him. His purity, his gentle spirit, his naked, candid ardour had enticed a like response from her. She had felt such tenderness for him, a tenderness which warmed her from within. She had reached a point where every part of Jason was desirable, where the shape of his knee, the minute hairs on the back of his hands, his moist, warm breath were all magnified, and hypnotically absorbing.

'Come on in, Jason,' she whispered, holding out her hand for him to take. She knew she would have to coax him in now that she had had her fun.

The poor boy hesitated. Emma stepped out into the backyard. The damp grass was spongy and her soft bare feet sank into it voluptuously. The natural sensuality of each step stimulated her senses and wakened her entirely from her unscheduled nap. She was reminded of Jason's kisses to her foot.

She stopped on the way to him and looked up at the half moon. The cool grass chilled her body, enlivening her. She wished to take off her clothes, the yoga pants which hung lazily to her hips, under which was nothing, and the hastily thrown on hooded sweatshirt. She had planned to dress for Jason, but her failure to do so had relinquished her of her responsibility to the program. What program? Hadn't this afternoon taught her anything?

Emma was feeling that feeling we all experience from time to time, of being utterly and unmistakably alive. Now she wanted to be naked. She was dimly aware that being so would propel her along the road with Jason further than she intended to go. But the feeling was overwhelming and being naked seemed so right and lovely on this moonlit midnight.

She looked across at Jason who had stepped out from his hiding place in the shadows of the azaleas. He was dressed as he was that afternoon. The light from the kitchen cast a soft glow over his features. His eyes were hungry for her, his lips were parted slightly, expectant, and he stood poised for action, fight or flight. She knew he could be up and over that fence to his left in one quick muscular moment. She had frightened him but the hunger remained in his eyes, the hunger that had caused him to defy his parents and David. His eyes were fixed upon her own now. She felt his desire.

Let him have me, she thought.

Under the light of the half moon in the middle of her back garden, near midnight, on the cool grass, in the crisp night air with her boy lover looking at her with a great, deep physical yearning, Emma recognised her true nature and with no thought given to her plans, lifted the light sweatshirt over her head. Before Jason had time to do or say anything, she dropped her yoga pants and stepped out of them and stood, for the first time, completely naked before him.

Emma closed her eyes and raised her hands above her head as the night air wrapped itself around her, thrilling her with its cool touch. Opening her eyes she seemed to salute the moon before looking back to her lover who was, understandably, elated at this sudden change in her.

He made no move to her though. She stood watching him, trying to keep his eyes on hers, but with no success. His roamed over her, shooting up to her face for reassurance, then leaving it to run amok over the length and slight breadth of her lovely body. His palpable excitement was so arousing to Emma. She'd never experienced the like.

Men move so swiftly. The boy drank her down in great gulps for he believed the cup was bottomless, that her beauty was bottomless. Men assume too much. To some of them, one woman is much like another, and in their haste they forget to look, really look, before taking her in their arms. But dear Jason knew nothing. He didn't know whether in a moment's time Emma would dress and kiss him goodnight. He didn't know if he'd ever see her naked again. He knew nothing of her body, and wanted to know, but felt time was slipping away and so took her in greedily. The more he looked at her the more beautiful she became, the more he desired her, the more he wanted this moment to last. Still he stood metres from her and made no move towards her.

Emma couldn't move either. The pressure of his gaze held her firmly to the spot. True, she wanted to be touched, she wanted to be kissed, she wanted to be held, but this new experience was compelling. She felt shy before his eyes and was blushing in the moonlight.

Finally he took a step. His eyes kept her standing still. He didn't step towards her, he stepped to the side and began to circle her ever so slowly. The night air was chilling but the warmth of her body's burning pride was countering it. He made her feel the most beautiful woman in the world. The feeling for her was one of overwhelming happiness, extraordinary pride and warm arousal. Her whole body was tingling, her nipples stood erect, she was very wet and warm between her legs. She was aware of every part of her body; her skin was violently alive to each sensation from within and without.

His gaze left marks upon her. He had made his way behind her now and she could feel his eyes as they wandered up and down the length of her. She felt them cup her butt. She wanted to bend over for him, to expose to him one area he had little chance of seeing as she stood. But his eyes seemed, even now, to keep her upright and still.

As Jason completed his circle of admiration he came very close to her side. She kept her eyes forward and let him bring his mouth to her neck. He was behind her now. The warmth of his body was against her, sending a chill through her, giving her goose bumps. She could actually sense his hesitation. To touch or not to touch, the poor boy seemed to ask.

FIFTEEN

Emma was delighted by his hesitation, showing him still firmly enthralled by her, physically and mentally. He respected her, and admired her and, it must be said, feared her. Not only was her body new to him, mesmerising and desirable, but her mind kept him fascinated and wanting more. Teach me, his actions seemed to say. Lead me by the hand.

Disturbing her thoughts, Jason spoke in a breathless murmur.

'Every part of you . . . Emma. Thank you. You are so beautiful,' he managed to say, before leaning forward and resting his lips lightly on the nape of her neck. Again a moan escaped her. She closed her eyes. She felt one hand cup her breast and the other warm moist hand rest on her bottom, lightly at first then gripping her more forcefully. His fingers teased her nipple very gently, it might have been his mouth. His kisses on her neck grew more heated and Emma leant against his mouth and gave way to him.

He took her in his arms at long last, and spun her round to face him. The heat from his body met her cool skin and she shuddered against him. He lifted his mouth from her neck and turned his eyes upon hers before kissing her mouth with warm open lips.

His hands took the place of his eyes and roamed up and down her back, caressing her gently till they reached her bottom which seemed to encourage more enthusiastic caresses. Both of his strong hands kneaded her, a cheek each, while their mouths were pressed together, their tongues meeting again and again in lovely embraces.

Emma's arms were around him but soon they came between them and, throwing caution to the wind, she began unbuttoning his jeans. There was no mistaking his desire for her; she felt him hard against her. She wanted to release him, to take him in her hands, to feel the warmth of him against her naked body.

She paused in her attempts to unbutton him, thinking it more urgent to do away with his t-shirt. She lifted it up. They broke their kiss and he stepped back and lifted the shirt over his head. He let it drop to the grass, seizing her again, his naked chest against her breasts. Her hands were not to be denied though. They forced their way between them and undid that top button at last. The other buttons, happy to oblige, sprang open jubilantly. The hipless Jason hindered gravity not at all and so these jeans fell about his ankles immediately.

Emma now had no reservations about taking the boy in hand, but she did like to enjoy herself. His kisses became even more ardent, seeming to suggest she might like to run speedily on to her object. He pressed himself against her hand to reiterate. But Emma could feel the long, thick shaft of Jason's painfully erect penis well enough through the light cotton weave of his boxer shorts. She knew, from that first day, how easily she might have him reaching orgasm. She knew too that since that first day she had not once given him the same pleasure. In fact Emma had regretted being so obliging that first day and this was why now she again paused on the brink.

She took hold of his shaft through the boxer shorts, that much she would do. She felt it pulsate under her grip. She even stroked it once. Jason jolted. His kisses stopped and he stared at her. She squeezed hard. She sensed the onrush of the orgasm. She let go.

She suddenly thought better of herself.

'Don't move,' she demanded of him, before rushing into the house.

Jason stood near naked, as naked as he was that day he came in search of his tennis ball. He looked about him for the first time since Emma had disrobed. He was startled by the audacity of them both, as if he was not one of them. He could see the back of his parents' house, but no windows. He looked to the other neighbour, no windows could be seen there either. But when he checked Emma's house there were four darkened windows upstairs facing him and the dark windows of the back room and the lit windows of the kitchen. David might be watching him now.

The kitchen lights went off.

Emma came out of the darkness carrying two

rugs. She felt so cheeky rushing around nude in his presence. This was her backyard. They were her deckchairs. Her husband was asleep upstairs, she'd run up to check on him. She held the rugs to her body and took a look at her young lover. He made her feel so naughty, so excited and hungry. She knew what she would do now and she could hardly wait. She kissed Jason and then threw down one of the rugs on the grass.

'Lie down, beautiful boy,' she said, as she knelt on the rug. 'Are you cold?'

'No,' he replied, and he did as he was told.

He lay down on his back. The moon became hidden by the large gum tree and he saw the immensity of space lit by a million stars. He didn't know what to do with his hands, he didn't know what to do at all. But he had little time to worry as Emma knew what to do. She lay her naked body on his and kissed the boy, deeply.

Jason now knew what to do. He took her head between his hands and messed with her thick dark hair, while holding her to his mouth.

Emma writhed over him, rubbing herself against him, his boxers still on, feeling his hard cock pressing against her, lifting herself up above its head and then resting her wet pussy against it.

Jason started. The warmth and softness, not to say wetness, was the first he knew of it and yet he knew it unmistakably. He thrust upwards slightly and she yielded to him. Was this to be it then? he asked himself, forgetting he was still wearing his boxer shorts. Emma's wetness had dampened his shorts so that it felt to both of them there was no impediment to further adventuring.

Emma ground down on him and he up against her. Both were lost now. There would be no going back. The pleasure felt, the closeness of their bodies, the hunger being fed, their kisses, deep and long, and his hands, his hands pressing against her head, rubbing her head, caressing her hair – no restraint now.

Emma broke from his kiss and looked into his eyes, saying, 'Be good now.' She started to kiss his chest, the soft young skin stretched across his developing pecs. She took in a nipple, teasing it, arousing a moan from him, biting it and then moving to the other. She found that both were very sensitive – she did like a man whose nipples were sensitive. Flicking his nipples and grinding on his hard-on was enough for her, but Jason continued to let his hands roam through her hair. She loved that. She could just lie still and have him do it, but knowing his hands were marking time with his pressing desire was even more pleasurable.

Emma's breasts hung freely, her head down, back bent, butt firmly placed, knees gripping him and her hips grinding her pussy against the head of his shaft. Each and every movement she made, sucking and biting one then the other of Jason's nipples, caused her breasts to sway slightly, dragging the tips across his warm flesh. These accidental touches were enough to generate the curious sensation of instant reciprocation. As her tongue flicked his hard warm nipple and she heard the boy moan she felt a delightful sensation in her own. His tender nipples, erect, moist and warmed by her tongue, and his cock, erect, moist and warmed by her pussy crowded her senses, satisfying, in tandem, both the giving and the taking aspects of her lovemaking.

Jason now had no claim to self-government. He was entirely under the sway of his Goddess, Emma. Her whims, her tongue, her amorous directives were unquestioned law to the boy. His body was not the body he had known hours before – minutes before, even. Since she had unceremoniously stripped off in front of him in the moonlight his body had teased him with sweet expectation. But his mind was unable to inform him of what he was to expect. His body was equal to the challenge; he drank in Emma's beauty, he luxuriated in the surprising revelation of her body and this behaviour suited her naked demands.

But it was a desperate action by Emma – when she pushed her hand between them – which took from Jason any hope of independence. Her hand and her hunger signalled a great change for him. Her desire was palpable and it was as unconditional as it had been conditional that afternoon. This unchecked hand and its aggressive progress was the greatest turn on Jason had ever experienced.

Quite naturally the boy felt his body swell and harden even more in response to her lust but unexpectedly, by reaching so hungrily for his cock, she was accepting him and yearning for him as a fully grown man.

She had brought into the moonlight his secret pride in his cock – his glorious, thick cock – and had confirmed the boy and made him man. The casual nature of youth with its fluctuating passions was lost back over that line across which

Emma had unwittingly dragged him. He gradu-
ated into manhood and, additionally, was made
a subject of desire, the desire for a woman, for
women.

SIXTEEN

Now, Jason had not yearned, as some do, for manhood. When he had swung over the garden fence that sunny afternoon a few days before, his greatest challenge was to pass his final exams. He had had his head down and was unaware that one could raise it and see the wide open world with all its contradictions and possibilities. Young Jess, who was very interested in Jason, had as yet failed to arouse in him an awareness of even her simple needs. Her effort was to try to coax from him exactly that which she was at great pains to hide. But Emma's impatience, carelessly and rather callously, caused him to hurdle, or more appropriately long jump, years of slow, young male development. If you could call the movement from boyhood to manhood progress, he had progressed.

Till now Jason's self-belief had been fuelled by academic and sporting successes and physical prowess. Because of this his position in the school hierarchy had been secure. He was left unmolested by more mature boys in his year, boys who had girlfriends or whose main concern was sex, or at least their concept of what sex was. They regarded him with a slightly mocking eye but his skill and strength had kept him from being openly derided. It was an all-boys' school, and he was far from the only virgin.

Jason's rapid sexual development was recognised by no one. His obsessive masturbation, his spiralling and distracting fantasies and his relationship with his neighbour were secrets of which he was ashamed. He would not boast of masturbation, he would not boast of Emma even though he detested secrets. He was a straightforward young man and a loving and obedient son but he was far from stupid and recognised the need for discretion and was learning quickly that life was anything but black and white. Pleasures brought with them some pain and much responsibility. But he was still unsure. He had much to learn.

Emma's lesson was continuing. The newly formed man was in flood. The pleasure wrought by tongue, hips, legs, hands, warmth, hair, wetness and her body's weight and that of her desire for him had burst the narrow banks of his youthful experience. Like the buoyancy one feels on entering the sea, Jason was lifted bodily by enrapturing sensation. Had Emma stopped, Jason would have gone to bed exhausted and slept without the need to masturbate.

But Emma did not stop. The woman was far too excited. She was finding the youthful flesh, the fresh salty taste of it, the scent of vibrant, bursting life too much for her. She sought to release him.

Earlier that night she'd not thought of being so accommodating, but what of it? She kissed his stomach, lifting her pussy from his throbbing cock head and sliding it along his thigh. His stomach flexed under her kisses and she ran her tongue across his tensed muscles. Her thrusting had not stopped, she pressed hard against his thigh with her hips. Finding no satisfaction she wriggled still lower till his knee fit snugly into her wet and messy region and she began, unceremoniously, to hump the boy's leg.

As her excitement grew, as her own orgasm evaded her, she found her focus was more and more centred on what was hidden by the unattractive boxer shorts Jason was wearing. They were wet and clung to him and in the moonlight she could see his erection jittering.

Jason's head was back and his eyes closed, his hands were still in Emma's hair but were caressing rather than possessing her. The boy moaned unrestrainedly and seemingly naturally.

How was Emma to resist? With her face up against his shorts she began to lift them. She ground against his knee and wished David would come out and fuck her too.

She saw for the first time the tip of Jason's cock. Her mouth was so close to it. She breathed out and blew hot, moist desire directly onto it. Reaching up, she rubbed her hand all over his stomach and chest. Her wicked tongue licked her lips and, as she brought her mouth to him, this wicked tongue darted out and licked the underside.

This action closed one door and op
and caused Jason to awake from one
enter another. He raised his head and
head over his groin. She glanced up at him. The
look in her eyes was nearly enough to cause the
reaction she was working for.

Jason had seen many sides to Emma thus far
but this debauched siren was new. She had had her
taste. Suddenly these eyes were lost to view under
a cascade of dark hair. She lifted the shorts still
further and dragged them down slowly.

The full length of his shaft came into her view.
She loved it at first sight and readily accepted full
and immediate ownership rights. Finders keepers.
It was longer and thicker than she had imagined
and she gripped it tightly with her left hand. It
pulsed dramatically against her palm. She had
little restraint, and contrary to art, contrary to
expectation, took the full length into her mouth.

The boy moaned as never before and Emma
thumped fiercely against his knee. She expertly
swallowed the entire length and breadth of his
warm shaft, sucked hard and then released.

Slowly, very, very slowly, and with all the pressure her tongue could muster pressed hard against
his shaft, she raised her head. The boy's hands

gripped her hair unmercifully and she felt him push her back down. This she readily assented to, but before he had time to acknowledge her acquiescence she was pumping that cock like a cheap pornstar.

The boy's hands fell from her head and clutched at the cool grass, ripping up handfuls. Emma's head bobbed up and down, sucking deep and long but releasing it just as quickly. The boy thrust his hips dangerously and Emma received the first warm gush. The scent was thick and burst into the air, and into her nostrils.

She continued sucking him and received another larger spurt and another and another till the boy became deathly still. The taste and its warmth, not forgetting the sheer volume, delighted her. Emma sucked on regardless. She knew what she was doing. He remained hard as she sucked and she was delighted to witness Jason beginning to tense again.

She'd banked on the virility of youth and she found she was not to be disappointed. Soon the boy was gripping the grass once more. She took him in and out faster and faster, sucking harder and harder. Her pussy was throbbing and she was going mad with her need to be fucked, truly, meanly, cruelly fucked but she would not do it tonight. She sucked and thumped herself against his knee and was unable to climax.

The boy had no such trouble and soon Emma felt him tense and the second orgasm was wrenched from him. More come erupted into Emma's waiting and willing mouth. And again the boy died. But his cock, under Emma's constant attentions, showed no sign of failing her.

It was always a battle with her between the desire to be fucked and the desire to suck.

Many men, her husband included, took a long while to recover after one of her blow jobs. She liked to tease older men and make them fall completely under her spell. But all the energy that she built up in them, and finally released, knocked them around so much that they were as good as gone to her afterwards. A fact she was at once proud of and somewhat irked by.

But now, she had a partner she could suck and suck and suck and still fuck, if she so wanted to.

The cool air had begun to chill Emma but she had no desire to stop the fun she was having. She reached across with her other hand for the spare blanket and managed to drape some of it over her back. She was very much inclined to disregard, once again, her self-imposed order and climb up on board his lovely cock. His knee was not nearly as exciting as she imagined that shaft to be. But she also wanted to show this delectable young man to what lengths she would go to take him to levels of pleasure unheard of in his narrow experience. Unheard of, indeed, in many a man's wider experience. Emma knew where her talents lay.

Jason lay prone, unable to move, speak or think.

But his cock was full of life, it seemed to grow in Emma's tight grip.

Emma was feeling excessively possessive. She had never been with someone so young, she had rarely been with men under twenty-five. She usually found nothing sexy in young men. Older men, men who could lead her somewhere, men with pasts, men with money and freedom and that confidence only age can bring. But these men brought with them experiences quite different from this one. They brought with them imagination, eroticism and fabulous, fabulous technique, but they could not match the resilience of this young man.

Emma suddenly realised the full potential of this lover. All her ideas concerning Jason had been vague. She had thought idly of teaching him. But now she saw what benefit to herself this education might bring. She imagined a young man, she imagined this young man, and his cock, equipped with a brain full of exceptional learning. Technique coupled with youth. Mmmm, her mind bubbled over. It was even more difficult to restrain herself. She yearned for his cock to fill her up. But . . . But . . .

She took him back into her mouth, deep-throat, banishing selfish desire in favour of the long-term benefits good planning could bring.

She was not so benevolent this time around though. She actually ached for release. As she sucked she snuck her hand underneath and began to fuck herself, pushing four fingers and a thumb in. She liked to do this when her whole body seemed to have crossed over some line and thought itself unsatisfiable. The shock of so much entering into so little was like a slap and usually rebooted her whole system.

Jason hadn't stirred and as she fucked herself she slowly and gently sucked him, holding him in her mouth.

She began to feel rising within her that sweet potential which is the harbinger of delight. Her mind was playing and playing and playing. Wicked thoughts enhanced her actions, as they always did. In her mind Jason rolled her onto her back, kissed her passionately and fucked her slowly and deeply.

In her mind Jason turned her around and bade her to sit on his face while she sucked him.

In her mind she was calling her husband down and in her mind he did and beat and fucked them both.

In her mind Jason woke from his stupor and forced her onto her knees, grabbed her hair in his hand and took her like an animal.

In her mind Jason's mother caught them and Emma orgasmed loudly on being seen as she really was.

In her mind Emma was quite disturbed! But then . . . aren't we all?

SEVENTEEN

The moonlit night was still and silent. The great gum above them barely stirred in the most breath-like of occasional breezes, no insects buzzed at the lovers' ears, and the distracted two would not have heard the very slight sound of the wavelets against the sand on the beach far below. The suburb slept soundly, or appeared to, for the blue flicker of TVs could be discerned here and there.

The only disturbance to be found was that sound made by our lovers. The hungry Emma growled and the recovering Jason moaned. Emma's hand had done its work, she was back. Her whole body shuddered to a familiar beat. She knew the road she was on but this didn't make the journey any less pleasurable. Her fingers were covered in the very wetness of her lust and she slid them over and around her lips, dipping now and then deep inside her but finally, after much teasing, they came to make circles on her demanding little clit.

Jason was recovering from the initial shock of what Emma had willingly done to him. He still lay back, eyes closed and inert but his mind was becoming clearer. He was close to tears of gratitude and love when he realised what she had done for him. It was a foolish response, he immediately thought, but the feeling bubbled up in him regardless of his male conditioning. He wanted to kiss her and hold her, he wanted to own her. His thought, My Emma, was the summation of his feelings.

Of course, his education had prepared him for such events. It came to the rescue with the truth. According to *The Young Male's Guide Book for Life* such behaviour was relegated to *whores* and *sluts,* of whom, the authors assured their readers, they had had much practical experience. Apparently, no decent woman would take a penis into her mouth. This indubitable understanding of the subject was in sharp contrast with Jason's own personal experience. But then the great book did not discourage such behaviour, not in the least, it actively encouraged it.

Intelligent and sensitive young men have much wrong information to overcome. In fact, all men do but only some seem willing to test the veracity of their knowledge; the others repeat the same nonsense to their peers, students and sons.

Jason was becoming aware, as the last few days will attest, that much of what he had previously known was to be discarded if he was to become the lover he now sensed he wanted to become. Creeping up on him was a new knowledge and this was not a slim one-volume affair, as was the case with *The Young Male's Guide Book for Life*. This new knowledge was boundless, and its volumes would fill the largest library many times over and would still remain unaccounted for in its entirety. This new knowledge was real life. The baffling enormity of human experience, and the abundant minutiae of human relations where the known is as daunting as the unknown, was now before him. It was for him that moment when we realise we are ever Life's student.

Poor young Jason was just recovering from his first experiences of oral sex and was still experiencing Emma's magic mouth – all the wonders of the world were crashing down upon him. But there were worse moments to have this realisation. He might have been alone and the weight might not have been borne. But he was not alone, he was at his most powerful and this weight was of little consequence, he managed it marvellously well.

Emma had been waking him, strengthening him, with each of her considered and most artful oral attentions. She was expert in the art of cock sucking. Her practical knowledge was extensive and she had stored within her memory many and various techniques to tantalise, tease and torment a man, to those oft-neglected pleasures only reached by toiling across the broad, dry plain of hopeless frustration.

The skilled sexual artist knows that each and every lover is unique and has needs different to all others and to achieve excellence takes time and much new learning. Emma knew that with Jason she wouldn't achieve that greatness only time can account for, but she would be able to take him out of himself and land him newborn upon the world. Such was her confidence.

All the while, sweet, sweet innocent Jason thought the tryst was ending.

Jason was wide awake and yet his eyes remained firmly shut. Emma could feel, as she played with him, thrills running through his flesh. He was becoming aware of every one of Emma's tiny ministrations. He lay quietly now, no moan, barely a breath and his body was tense. Thrill after thrill shuddered through him uncontrollably. He was not aware of what was happening. He felt all these things but this was so unlike anything he had experienced that he thought no more of it than that it was amazing. He thought she would raise her head at any moment and crawl up to him and kiss his lips. He wanted her to. He wanted to thank her. He wanted to take her into his body, somehow. To make her him.

Emma was quite lost in the moment. The brilliant stars millions of miles above them, the cool night air, the soft, moist, fragrant grass, the dark windows she knew to be behind her, the sleeping giant upstairs, the lovely young man beneath her, his wonderful, beautiful cock in her hand, in her mouth, in her hand, in her mouth and her other wicked hand playing, playing, playing, around, over, and on her clit, all mingled in mind and body, in sense and feeling, building a tower within her, which, when it had reached too high would come crashing down and send her mad with each wondrous, crushing, sensual blow.

When we think of Emma we remember her habits, one of those being her inclination towards postponement of pleasure in the greedy hope for more. Emma was determined to take Jason places unknown to him but she was just as determined to take herself to places unknown to her. She was capable of much at once. Hers was an instinctive sensuality tending towards outright greed. It was this greed which made her good, for she not only desired more for herself, she wanted more for others. She always wanted more.

So when she felt the tower wobble and incline towards pleasurable destruction, she removed her hand and the whole edifice vanished. The foreman stood by the foundation, dumbfounded but not defeated, he would begin the work again, cheerfully and with much vigour.

Jason's mind wandered off slowly, pleasure and expectation each taking a hand, leading him on a merry jaunt, keeping him distracted, while Emma played greedily with his body.

She had begun to stroke the length of his shaft slowly with her saliva-covered hand, her grip tight, like the boy's own would be, heedless of injury, and was all the while using her mouth on the underside of his balls. Sucking and licking his testicles, teasing his anus with her tongue, kissing and nibbling the upper reaches of his thighs. There was great timing to this, each stroke coincided with one of her forays below. She managed the boy's delight cruelly, for though she kept him hard and the thrills continued to shudder, she restrained his growing orgasm, treating him with contempt, holding him, bound and gagged in the basement of his growing tower. Such contempt is often a necessity when one is aiming high.

Emma's senses were flooding, her towers kept growing and growing, faster and faster, as the taste and smell of his come, still on her lips, on her hands, in her mouth, aroused in her primal, beastly, subhuman longing. She wanted so much for herself. Why couldn't David come down and fuck her? Why couldn't he sense her need?

But then the fear that he might do so stole her breath from her. Just imagine how the scene would appear from the window. From the kitchen door. Emma's arse raised, fingertips visible between her legs and her head buried in a man's crotch. And out in the open, on the lawn, completely nude, with no respect for her husband or the neighbours.

Just imagine the look on her drowsy, confused and cranky husband's face when he discovered who it was she was with. Would there be disgust? Would he finally crack? Jesus! Emma, you've gone too far. It's disgusting. You're perverted.

He probably wouldn't be able to speak. He might just turn around and leave.

Emma shuddered and her latest tower rocked heavily from side to side. The rocking became so perilous that the tower was forced to behave contrary to the laws of gravity for although it swayed dramatically it somehow managed to return, and Emma almost lost her mind.

She had removed her hand but Jason's scent, her fears and her husband's disgust were doing more than her fingers ever could. The tower would not crumble though. Her tolerance was draining from her and this tottering orgasm tower was such that the pleasure she received was becoming unbearable.

Her whole body jolted. And again. And again. If she didn't come now she never would. Every nerve in her body was firing, every muscle tensed and beginning to burn. Her breath had stopped. She was dying from pleasure. She always knew she would one day.

EIGHTEEN

Emma was forced into action by her inability to topple her tower. She once again pressed her hand into herself, but this time seeking and finding that much maligned and very real spot that has been so unimaginatively labelled. She began to rub the area like she might Aladdin's lamp. Impetuously, greedily, and somewhat thoughtlessly, contrary to the manner she found most favourable in saner times. This excited her all the more but failed to trigger the collapse she so desired. Her fucking husband could have done his bit! Was he lying asleep upstairs, dreaming wicked dreams, when his wife was living a wicked life? Come down and find out what kind of a woman you've married! Come down.

Her hand weakly and irregularly stroked Jason's cock. She stared hungrily at it though. She could feel it enter her. She wanted it entering her. She had to have it in her. There was no other way to topple her tower. But he had to take her.

Be a man, boy! Be a man! Can't you see what you've done to me?

She was on her knees and vividly imagining Jason on his knees behind her. No. Her husband. No. Jason.

The tower shook, her body shook, she hung on the edge, the edge of reason.

The power of the sensation was beginning to numb her senses. She forgot Jason. Only her husband in a full fury could bring her down. Fuck! Come on! Come on! Oh! Please, please. Oh fuck me! Fuck me! Your dirty whore of a wife! Fuck me! Her mind was spinning round and round this one hope. All of her body was pulled taut till spasms wracked her.

She needed to be caught. She needed to be caught! Now!

She pressed her head against Jason's thigh as

her hand squeezed his thick shaft and felt the first heavy thud of her husband's hips against her arse as he embedded himself in her.

She felt his hand on her neck, gripping it roughly. He was swearing at her. Calling her all the worst names a husband could conjure up.

He lifted her head and made her take the boy's cock in her mouth. The whole length of it disappeared and he held her there. She was choking. Her eyes watered. But she sucked it for her husband.

He wanted her to be all that she was. The demeaning deluge of vile words kept rolling from his vicious tongue. She was pushed forward by David's heavy, hard thrusts, thumping deep, deep inside her. He hated her at this moment. He was so hard, a truncheon. He brutalised her. Criminal wife! Pounding her hard and fast. He wanted to climax in her one last time. He'd leave her for this. No fucking respect. But he also knew his wife so well, and wanted to leave her knowing just what she was forfeiting. The glutton. She didn't marry me for nothing. He lowered his hips slightly and thrust up and found what she had been looking for all this time. Dynamite!

'Emma! What the hell are you doing?'

There it was! The tower toppled. She lifted her head, arching her back, leaving Jason's cock. She let out an unchecked, deep moan, too loud for the backyard at midnight. Her whole body shook uncontrollably. She collapsed onto him and quaked violently, her hand still in herself, her sex pulsating, tears in her eyes. She began crying in earnest. The aftershocks were delicious. The first wave had been too intense for her conscious self to acknowledge, let alone judge, but these tremors were absolutely divine. The feeling enveloped her, she became the feeling. She was this pleasure, all other aspects of her life were meaningless. She lay inert, still crying, her body trembled, her skin felt the cold air, the warmth of their bodies, the pressure of Jason's hand caressing it; in short, her skin hummed and her ears heard nothing but the blood surging in them.

'Are you OK?' Jason was asking, in a frightened voice. To his eyes, Emma looked to be sobbing. Now she was upset! What had he done? He had been dragged back from a land of delight by Emma's extraordinary behaviour. She had been swearing at herself. Calling herself names and then choking herself on his cock. He hadn't seen her hand working at herself relentlessly. He hadn't felt what she had felt. He hadn't access to Emma's fantasies. He had no idea a woman could do what Emma had just done.

Jason just lay caressing her. The poor woman was beside herself, he thought. She continued to cry, so he pulled the blanket over her and let her cry.

Emma had rarely orgasmed like that. She had been brought to tears so few times in her life. The exhaustion she was feeling was complete. She'd been close for so long and the orgasm itself had gone on and on and lingered still. She felt the echoes and phantom orgasms as though in a dream. Her body was just releasing the tension the most efficient way it could. The tears flowed, hot and wet. She would often marvel at the variety of orgasms she could experience. That was the most tense, irritating and tormenting bugger of a build up. And the orgasm itself! Her whole body was vibrating. She'd be sore tomorrow, no doubt. It was a work-out.

She dozed off . . .

She woke with a start.

'Jesus! How long was I asleep?' she asked, somewhat breathlessly.

'You were asleep?' he replied.

'How long have I been lying here?'

'A minute, two. I don't know.'

'Are you alright?'

'I'm sorry, Emma. I didn't know what I was doing.'

'What? What? Oh, darling. Mmmmm. Baby. I just came, that's all. You did nothing wrong. You did everything right.'

Emma crawled up to his mouth and kissed him tenderly and long. She felt him stiffen against her.

'But you were crying,' he said disingenuously, suddenly proud of himself and ashamed of his pride.

'That's the power of your hot young cock. Thick, long, powerful young cock. I love it. I love your hard,' she gripped it, 'thick, beautiful cock. It's mine.'

She kissed him again. Their tongues were on the same beat, their bodies, hands and desires were entwining again. Emma's exhaustion had revealed the bare skeleton of her energies and she was inclined to waste these too. Every touch was enabling her to revisit the past. She felt such love for Jason. She wanted him to know just how much she wanted him, how much she appreciated him and how beautiful she thought him.

Her hand was between them, gripping him, her

tongue was with his, her body rubbed itself against him. The warmth of their bodies was sweet to her, their shared warmth.

Jason was caressing her bum when he made the warm wet discovery. His fingers slipped on Emma's come. It was everywhere and it excited him terribly. He rubbed it all over her arse cheeks, kneaded them. But he kept away from the darker regions between them. She could feel him tentatively explore then retreat. She was amazed at the way his inexperience still kept him at bay after all they had done together. He was ever the good boy! He had never touched her there. How she wished he might now!

She wiggled her bum provocatively and moaned for him. She wondered what he might do if his fingers found her arsehole. Could you just feel those blind fingers timidly scouting the forbidden region unaware of the erotic implications? She could almost hear his thoughts as he roamed the known regions of her arse, wondering at the unknown reaches between the lovely fleshy cheeks. He wanted to be there. She knew that. His explorations grew steadily more daring but still remained a distance from his unnamed desire and her named one.

Emma, in the midst and during this long slow aftermath of her orgasm, had forgotten her original aim. She would have readily admitted to herself that she would have to try to give the boy the blow job of his life some other time. She was spent. But she was aware that he was not. His cock pulsated in her hand. It felt hot. It was hot.

All the while their mouths had continued a glorious, meandering kiss, the kind of kiss that is somnolent, more dream than actuality. Their thoughts were fluid, finding their ways under doors and through cracks, dripping and pouring into regions untrammelled by daily concerns. Two tongues, four lips and a million miles of wide open spaces. Jason loved these kisses. He loved to kiss Emma. She always put so much into her kisses. He thought she was never more eloquent than when kissing. He could learn more from one of Emma's dreamy kisses than from all of his schooling.

But then he felt a change in her. She was readying herself for a goodbye. He could tell. He'd faced so many goodbyes from her. She was always having to break away from his kisses. Jason could kiss for ever. Emma always kissed between appointments.

NINETEEN

Jason wouldn't let her go tonight. They had till dawn. What did they need sleep for? He held her tightly, rolled her over and lay on top of her. Emma was so surprised she let out a sweet little sound of alarm. He had her beneath him now. He seemed bigger somehow, bulkier, more man than boy. How he had grown! His weight when clothed and safe and just a teenage boy, kissing her on a sunny afternoon, had seemed paltry compared to the weight of her husband. But now, naked, hard, dangerous, with menacing intent, he seemed heavier, more masculine, stubbornly powerful.

All the come in the air, in her mouth, on her hands, on the blanket and all over them, this male scent was stripping what she knew of him and revealing what he was. An adult male.

She had automatically raised her knees. The man he'd become knew what she wanted. Her pelvis shifted and he felt her pussy for the first time. It was pressed against his shaft. Her lips were so wet and soft. Were warm. He too shifted his pelvis and his shaft slid along her lips and he grew so very excited.

He started to pant and, staring into Emma's eyes in disbelief, slid his cock back up along her very wetness.

'No, darling. No,' she managed to say, breaking from one of the most suggestive kisses of her life. He was telling her, using a kiss to do so, what he wanted. If he'd done it, if he'd done it! But no. He had to ask. Damn, damn, damn!

She tried to move him off her. She couldn't make him budge. He looked into her eyes. She had resolve. He saw it. She tried to move him. He wouldn't. His cock slid on her lips. He was looking, quite blindly, for something he had never searched for before. His cock head passed right over the entrance to his future. But it wandered too far and passed over it again on the return trip. Emma was delirious. Still her eyes told him no. And still her hands tried to move him off her.

That thick cock of his was discovering other places now. The full weight of him seemed to be present behind him when he came to rest on her swollen clit.

Still her eyes said no. Her legs, on the other hand . . . They squeezed the boy, the man. Oh, just thrust blindly! Just trust instinct and let your worries go. I need to feel the full width of you in me now! Open me up! I'm willing to be taken. I won't have it any other way.

Suddenly the boy returned and he rolled off her and lay on his side. His hand ran over her stomach, his fingers marking figures along her moist skin. He cupped her left breast, then her right. Emma felt the cool night air of her skin and also felt the sadness of a missed opportunity. She could but look forward to the day when he might take her and she him without reserve. All these games. All this inhibition and inexperience. But she must be gentle.

She could see his cock standing erect and wanted it so very much but felt powerless. Somehow she knew just how it should be. She was the older woman, she was the experienced entity. She had responsibilities to him even though she shrugged off the responsibilities to state, husband, neighbour and friend. That meant she had more of a responsibility to do the best by the boy. In one move she could steal his right to future initiative.

While thinking such thoughts his hand did something. In one full, swift movement from breast to pussy, Jason gambled a future of maybes against a present of certainty. She was naked beside him *now*. That was all he knew. He may never have the chance again. He truly felt that.

His fingers were all over her, rubbing her lips, playing with them, curious, sliding on the wetness and then slipping into her. It all happened so quickly. Jason's eyes were opened wide. He was peaking. He could feel an orgasm building. His fingers were inside her. He hadn't put in one. No. He hadn't put in two. No. Three fingers had slid easily into her. Emma had arched back immediately.

To her, this inexperienced teenager's overstatement was a very welcome shock to her system. And it was a shock to have three fingers unexpectedly enter even when she was drenched and willing, and when she was debauched, and when she had only recently brought herself to a shattering climax. It still came as a shock.

This wonder known as beginner's luck can sometimes be a harbinger of talent. But sometimes it is luck and only luck. For although Jason had heard mention of the clitoris and had a general sense of its importance to women, he was a little confused about its actual whereabouts. So when he felt a small lump between Emma's lips, and when this discovery exacted a positive response from her in the form of a low guttural moan, Jason, in all readiness, congratulated himself on having discovered it. He continued to massage it with his fingers and had the pleasure of seeing Emma writhing about and moaning.

He was being quite rough with her. But she was in no mood for the gentle touch. He fucked her now, with his fingers, watching his hand and her face alternately. His cock was bursting. His excitement was such that he felt sure he'd come all over her hip.

He began to hump her hip. But then he got a better idea. He climbed back on top of her, thoughtlessly removing his fingers from her and tried, in vain, to press his cock into her.

Emma found it very easy to get him off her this

time and she stood up, marking the end of their night.

She looked down at her lover who was not at all pleased by the sudden cessation of their play. He lay back on the rug, his cock lying large and erect against his body. A beautiful adonis, thought Emma as she looked smilingly down upon him. She picked up the other rug and wrapped it around her naked body. Jason caught one last view of her lovely full breasts and long milk-white legs.

She was unable to keep her eyes from his cock. She hated, truly hated leaving an erect penis. She thought she might just squat over it. Imagine that. Just to squat and have the thing enter her completely. Maybe she'd even turn her back on him and squat. Then it would be just her and the magnificent erection. Back to him. Cock slipping between her lips. She might squeeze tightly against it. No wait. She'd squat but slowly, slowly press it into her arsehole. Imagine that! The boy skips straight to buggery. Imagine that thick hard cock entering her there.

When it was that she dropped to her knees and began sucking again, only Jason knows for sure. Emma and her filthy mind had been too preoccupied to notice silly details like that. But there she was again, arse raised, head down, blowing the boy like the cheapest of cheap whores.

The boy blew into her mouth, his body convulsing and two half-suppressed moans escaping to be lost in the quiet night air.

While Jason lay in the aftermath of this orgasm Emma let the taste of him and the smell of him permeate her senses. She kissed his now flaccid cock with wet lips and tongue and rubbed her wet fingers into his pubic hair. She lay in the sweet regret of having finally sated his young cock. She consoled herself with the knowledge that, from now on, day after day, night after stolen night, it was hers to play with. In her mind she began to reorganise her week around his cock.

While thinking of stealing moments with Jason, Emma took the whole of it in her mouth again. She was just playing, loving the taste and had no further designs on it. She was thinking of the pleasures of teaching the boy how to kiss her between her legs and then thinking of whole afternoons spent sixty-nineing in the manner of their first afternoon spent kissing. She was imagining them coming and coming. What over-indulgence!

Thinking this and playing thus immoderately with his flaccid penis she was surprised to feel the stirring of a new life. She kept it in her mouth and his cock grew and grew, pushing itself deep into her, until it was as hard as ever. Emma realised she'd never get any sleep tonight.

What was she to do? she wondered at the time. The longer she was away from her husband's side the greater the chance of him waking and wondering where she was at such a late hour. And poor Jason. The young perform badly on little sleep. She imagined him at school the next day. She shuddered at the thought of this man being squashed back into the uniform of the boy. What had she done?

But he was in her mouth and she was now sucking again.

Surely the night was still young, came a reassuring voice from within Emma's psyche.

You've only just begun, said another.

Why not remove the boy wholly from the nursery? spoke a third.

Sit on the boy. Fuck him! I'm tired of your games. Enjoy your prize to the full. Stop playing with your food, young miss, demanded a fourth.

Were there no dissenting voices in Emma's head? Where were the sensible voices? Where was her conscience? Or were these the voices of her conscience? They did seem to speak sensibly. They did have their points.

The temptation to lift herself and sit on this marvellous cock seemed such a slight temptation but for Emma it was becoming one of the greatest she'd yet faced and resisted. She mustn't take him. He must take her. She mustn't hand everything to him. A hand-fed, tame beast would be no fun, no fun at all.

Her resolve returned as Jason began to moan. She stopped sucking and stood up. She distracted herself by becoming busied in dressing. Once dressed she looked down upon her lover and her legs weakened. Turning her head to the house she scanned the blackened windows then determined to gather up Jason's clothes for him.

Jason lay watching Emma. His desire for her was the strongest it had been all night. She was sending him off home. She was pretending to have returned to normal, more normal than she had ever been, in fact. The way his cock felt, the blood having returned, hardening it, pushing into the exhausted cock, the strange pain of it, made him proud. He was reclining on an elbow, naked, whilst Emma stood dressed, holding out his clothes to him, eyes averted. His erection seemed to him to be harder and larger, with that burning sensation one gets when you stretch a sore muscle. Emma wouldn't look at it. He saw that and liked her behaviour. His cock actually throbbed.

'Time for bed,' she said in a strange voice. She was unable to look at him. Jason made no move. He was watching Emma intently and actually saw she was fighting the temptation to keep going. This was not natural behaviour for her and it showed. She was awkward and inhibited. She steeled herself and turned her face to him and handed over the jeans and boxer shorts.

'Come on . . . Get dressed. We've had fun, don't ruin it,' she said, while thinking herself an ass. She was trying so hard to be a wet blanket. The part didn't suit her, she was over-reaching, her acting wasn't up to it and she had certainly failed to convince her audience. Jason felt sure he'd have her in his arms in no time. He lifted his hand and tugged at her pants. She looked down at him and their eyes met. He was different.

'Let go, Jason. It's late,' she said, stepping back from him but he held on tightly to the loose cotton. The pants came down along her thigh. Jason saw her pussy again. A forceful desire stamped impatiently within him and he pounced, dragging his prey down onto the ground.

He ripped off her pants. His hard, young, naked body wrapped itself around Emma and she was overpowered in barely a blink of the eye.

He lay on top of her again, held her, pressed his cock against her mound and his mouth against hers. He kissed her roughly, deeply, and she clung on to him.

Emma's whole body trembled, she raised her knees, spread herself and kissed Jason with a manic hunger. Anyone who chanced upon them now would have said they had just begun. They kissed as two lovers long separated finally united. Jason made no attempt to press his cock into her. She made no attempt to help him. Both hungered for consummation.

Though Jason truly felt he was forbidden to go that one step further, his body was insistent he try. He was painfully erect. The pleasures running through all of his senses seemed to urge, to urge, to urge. But it must be remembered that the urging came with no instructions. And Emma had said no. He remembered how he'd felt sliding along the soft, wet folds. He'd masturbated with oil, with cream, with soap, with pre-come

and come but . . . He knew what happened. He'd
seen diagrams and pictures. He knew how to do
it! He knew it!

Emma would welcome him. She was so very
ready for him. She lifted her pelvis again. She
couldn't help herself. He began to thrust ever so
slowly. The whole of his lower body moved against
her, met her lift. But he didn't move his cock from
her mound and their kissing, manic, violent, deep,
continued.

TWENTY

Now it was Jason's turn to lie. He leapt off her. Stood naked and erect above her.

'You're right, Emma, it's late,' he said with a grin. He hoped she'd think he was teasing but the truth was, he realised he couldn't do it. He was frightened. He suddenly doubted he could actually go through with it.

A sharp, uncomfortable pain entered his head. An ugly doubt. What if he was a poor lover?

He reached for his jeans, pulled them on and stuffed his boxers into his pocket.

Emma lay on the grass, panting like a animal.

She couldn't believe it frankly. She was sure the time had come and her will was to be overturned. But in a flash the beautiful body was gone. She watched him pull on his top. I can stand it, she thought.

'Well . . . if you're tired . . . I wouldn't want to keep you up,' she said, rising slowly to her feet. She stepped back into her pants. He was already moving to the fence. She thought that was just a little too provoking.

'You've had your fun and you're just going to leave . . . and not even kiss me goodnight?' she said, stepping slowly across the cold grass towards him.

Poor Jason was so young, so old and so divided. The beast within him had not been sated even after all Emma had done for him. In fact, all of her attentions had only served to roll away the stone and let the true primal spirit out. When he turned to look at her, his eyes had an unnerving presence of mind.

'Don't tease me, Emma,' he said.

'Are you just going to leave?' she asked, coming up close to him.

'You want me to go.'

'Yes, I do,' she said. She reached up and brought

his mouth to hers, kissed him, and whispered, 'Go.' She took hold of his hand and slowly, keeping his eyes on hers, led it under the elastic of her yoga pants. She placed his warm hand on her wet lips. He pressed two fingers into her immediately. She let his fingers play for a moment then withdrew his hand and put his fingers to his mouth and he was made to lick them.

'Goodnight, sweet prince,' she said with a smile, and turned to walk away.

Our personal behaviour, our individual character, has such a short history while more elemental human behaviour has a history spanning millions of years. This human behaviour is very sure of itself. Its aims may appear shallow or shortsighted at times but it evolved when the world was less complicated, when life was nasty, brutish and short. All of our intellectual pretensions, our civilised inhibitions, our stumbling, fumbling empathies and our casual nods towards the rule of law seem at times to be impediments to our true state of being.

Jason was made aware of this ancient truth by the sudden turning away of the woman he desired. Nothing short of armed intervention would have prevented him from acting on impulse. As she stepped away she triggered a response in him at once frightening and relieving. And yet, in some dark corner of Jason's mind was the dim acknowledgement of her consent. Theirs was a play and counter play of dumb beasts dressed in their modern finery. All of the urgency of the past few hours met with and welcomed the overdue quantity of bloody determination which was so evidently lacking till now.

Miss Mischief herself had a feeling she had planted a seed that would ripen overnight. She immediately pictured the boy rushing home to help himself over that last hurdle before collapsing into bed, thoroughly, utterly exhausted. She assumed he'd awake with a determination to fuck her and she imagined him chasing her down at the first available moment.

This was the instant line of thought buzzing through her mind, a thought she was to use up in bed beside her husband. She would have easily imagined escaping from Jason's clutches, teasing him, not letting him fuck her. She might have visualised them stark naked running the length and breadth of her lovely home till finally, bruised and battered, she would have surrendered her body to the boy and would have had him ravish her again and again till every ounce of him was spent.

But Emma was to be disappointed in this for now her genius for prophesy was blocked by a new and startling entity: Jason's newborn will. This would add another element to their relationship – chaos.

There was one thing, one thing only that Jason wanted to do. He saw it, clear as day. He knew exactly what he was doing and the effect it would have and he was loving the knowledge.

He took hold of Emma's wrist and she turned casually, ready to make some glib remark till she saw the smile on his face. She suddenly felt the real fear of the weaker nature when the codes of civilisation are stripped roughly away by a savage.

Fight or flight? Her body chose the latter but Jason's hand held her firmly by the back of the neck. With his other he undid his jeans, let them fall and stepped out of them.

Emma's initial fright merged, under the direction of her many perversions, with excitement as her yoga pants were yanked from her.

'No, Jason!' she said, the words escaping from her lips, expressing her fear but creating in their turn a greater fear – that he might take heed of them.

But he hardly heard them. She struggled to get

free to no avail. Hadn't she wanted a wild animal? Nothing she could do would stop him. His grip on her neck was very tight, he was hurting her and forced her to relinquish her will to his. She once again felt his cock against her. They were both standing, her back to him, his cock pressed against her butt, one hand on her neck, the other on her hip.

The sight of Emma's arse was further cause for his primal intoxication. He pushed up her top and admired her back. Then he yanked the top over her head and gripped her neck once more.

He admired too his domination. He pulled off his own top so that they were both properly attired. He was rigid. He made one exploratory pass with his cock, running the length of her wet lips before finally, with no trumpets, no fanfare, thrusting deep inside her.

The two of them moaned simultaneously and similarly. Two deep and extended Ohs, expressing relief, pleasure and, for Emma, the satisfaction of having him enter her on his terms.

Jason stood for a moment embedded in his woman, savouring this new delight, so unlike any he had yet experienced and yet so familiar. A mere moment to savour, for the blood rushing in his temples urged him to action. He began to fuck the woman who dragged him from his teenage slumbers. Emma was completely under his control, he held her so surely there was no escape, nor now the will to. He thumped himself into her without restraint. He seemed ever incited to fuck her with greater force. A brutality surged through him from some deep previously untapped reservoir.

Emma was being thrown around by each thrust. His two great forces, his powerful young hand pulling her to him and the greater power of his hips battering her were uneven. Emma began to moan uncontrollably. Each thrust of his was entering hard and deep and he was thrusting faster and faster with no sign of failing. Emma began to feel herself depart under all this power. She was being truly taken. He pounded her with no care. Unrestrained. The desire to climax his only goal and thanks to Emma's mouth that goal was a long, long way off.

Jason was lost in the power and the glory, lost to the pleasure of rule. His senses were filling with the sounds of Emma's moans, the scent of her, which wafted up to him, the visual splendour of this beautiful woman in his hands, her round, pert butt, her obvious pleasure, his handling of her. He was a god.

But they stumbled forward. Even a god can thrust too hard, too far for his own restraining hand. He caught her up before they both went headlong into the garden.

Wise Emma took precautions, protecting the precious fuck she was experiencing from farce by reaching up and grabbing the top of the fence. Jason moved with her and without a break in their play, the two were steady and now Jason could truly find just how hard he could fuck his lover.

Jason gripped Emma's hips, taking hold of the lovely soft flesh he found and began to experience for the first time what all the fuss was about. The pleasures of the flesh experienced as flesh in flesh.

Against flesh.

Base, urgent, lust.

To be a witness to the arch in Emma's back, her pale, flawless skin in the soft moonlight, the indented line of her spine running all the way down and between a delicious pair of dimples before disappearing in the rise of her perky butt . . .

To witness her legs, long, slender, stretched taut for she was up on her tippy-toes, slightly spread, serving to present herself to her lover . . .

To witness her head dropped forward, her hair everywhere and the two lovely arms reaching up to the top of the fence where her hands met and held on . . .

To hear her moan . . .

To witness all this might well have been enough for any man.

Jason was privileged, he felt privileged and more than that . . . for she was his tonight.

There are those who say to be a good lover one has to lose oneself totally *in the moment*. But can that be true? For Emma, fucking was all about being aware. Being aware of her partner's needs, what turns them on, what most probably will if only they'd try . . . Being aware of their limits too, and of their fears, but also being aware of the effect she'd have on her partner. She had no illusions. She knew instinctively how to move to keep a man's attention, what poses cause a man to faint, just how erotic she could be. It excited her to know.

The pose called for by the situation and her own subtle understanding worked not only to turn Jason on but the pose was one which excited her terribly. She knew how she looked and her vanity, her own pride in the way she looked, coupled with the pleasure she was giving made her tremble. If Jason were to step back and just watch her, she felt she might be able to come just from the sweetness of her own self-love and his love.

Jason was not yet a good lover, he was lost in the moment. These sensations he was experiencing for the first time. Jason was lost to his fucking, for this was fucking pure and simple. All of his fears had gone. His mother's head popping up over the fence would not have caused him to miss a beat. He'd have continued through any crisis for he no longer cared about anything but the fuck. Emma could not have planned this better, the boy had even forgotten his elusive orgasm. There was no goal for the boy. To fuck or not to fuck? To fuck . . . no doubt.

He had her hips, he heard her moans, he had the power, he knew nothing of her needs, nor cared. He gripped and thrust hard and deep, ever faster and harder. The stamina of the fit young sportsman and the strength of him were a wonder. He always seemed to be able to find more power to use. He knew no limits as it was his first time.

And what of Emma? Can it be possible you don't know?

The whole neighbourhood could hear her now. That is, if they weren't indifferent or asleep or crouching close to an infomercial.

Surely someone peered out of a window, hoping to catch sight of the offender, ears cocked, listening to the wild sounds of a woman under the sweetest of attacks? For although there was no doubt that the sounds were an expression of pleasure and their rhythmic nature denoted actual fucking going on, the listener might consider such unchecked pleasure an offence. For they were not the recipient.

Life in the suburbs has much to teach. It can teach you how to limit yourself so that you appear no better or worse than your neighbour, for being better would be downright unneighbourly. It teaches you to enjoy yourself, but moderately. Sure, have a party, but we'd like two weeks' warning and we will call the police at ten past eleven if we hear a sound, especially the sound of fun being had. But suburbia cannot help you live. It cannot help you when you stumble upon a pleasure that just makes you scream, that makes you want to sacrifice all of your other values to it.

And Emma was there now. Not that she was ever, inwardly, much of a conformist but she did keep up appearances. It was easier. At that moment though she was no longer of the suburbs. The young man's marvellous cock was causing mischief. It was blowing away the smothering detritus left by civilisation constantly rubbing against her nature.

Her moans, her cries, were not checked for she no longer had such considerations.

Was she inconsiderate? Damn right! In the truest sense. His deep thrust was finding that place, the sweet, sweet hidden pleasure spot, so few cocks have the temerity to find. Try to stifle yourself when a cock finds that spot! And be damned if you do for it would be wrong! Wrong, wrong, wrong! Just how many lives do you think you have to live?

Had David appeared she would have been able to say with utmost clarity (after climbing down, a stiff drink and a long, warm, scented bath) – I love you but I would not have missed that pleasure for the world. And further, if you loved me as I love you, you'd never want me to miss such pleasure . . . ever.

The two lovers were in the midst of one of those much sought-after couplings wherein each partner is afforded a level of pleasure each believes is greater than the pleasure the other receives.

Each selfish thrust of Jason's fed his hunger and gave him great pleasure.

Each selfless thrust of Jason's fed Emma's hunger and gave her great pleasure.

Whereas Jason was running down a delinquent orgasm, tirelessly, Emma was believing him to be dodging and weaving as an orgasm tried to run him down.

The balance was well in Pleasure's favour.

Jason's panting, interspersed by his low, guttural growls were well matched by the breathless gasps from Emma's wide open mouth. Jason was sweating now and his whole body began to gleam in the moonlight. The tanned body was tensed so that each muscle was easily definable. Caught thus, his age would be harder to guess at. He was a man in the moonlight, naked and fucking intently. His powerful form in action was all man. His jaw set as it was, confirmed a very adult determination. But that was not all, for the very veins in the back of his hands as they gripped Emma, fingers splayed; the muscles in his forearms and his broad shoulders; those calves too, cyclist's calves, and his thick powerful rugby thighs, well they were all fully formed, they were all the stuff of an adult male – a base, physical, brutal animal male made to fuck.

And fuck he did.

TWENTY-ONE

Emma slept soundly, spread wildly across her beloved bed. Unbeknownst to our heroine, a bright and lively summer's day beat a vibrant tune against the shutters. And it would continue to beat unacknowledged for some time, for the woman was spent and her body was recharging.

Hours ago now, David had climbed heavily out of bed, sure of disturbing his beautiful wife and receiving a lovely sleepy look from her as he readied himself for his shower. But no such smile came this particular morning. Emma was immovable. He could see she was nestled in the arms of a deep sleep. He shook the bed unnecessarily. She didn't stir.

He had no memory of the previous night's grumpy mood, sleep had made him a new man. In any case, the mood he had taken to bed had had nothing whatsoever to do with his life with Emma.

If he had thought more about it he may have come to the erroneous conclusion she was angry at him for his mood, but he hadn't that kind of mind. He assumed instead that she had been reading till late. He couldn't remember if she had said anything to him about having assignments or essays due. But seeing he couldn't remember her coming to bed at all he assumed she was tired from burning the candle at both ends again. He was only opposed to her studies when they made her too tired to spend the little time they had together effectively.

So accordingly, having received no morning smile, no teasing request to stay in bed, no forward, erotic advance that he'd have to reject anyhow, he rose in a grumpy mood which the shower quickly washed from him.

He returned to the bedroom after having a rushed bowl of muesli and stood by the bed with a coffee in his hands, sipping it slowly while appreciating the beauty of his wife.

Earlier, while he had dressed, Emma had not moved. He had almost opened the shutters to let the day in. But now David saw that the sleeping Emma had noticed his absence and had acted accordingly. She lay spread generously over the whole of the bed. David smiled at this when he might have taken offence. He might have taken this action as analogous to their life together, but he didn't. He saw the nature of his wife, the very nature which thrilled him. She was extravagant whilst he was cautious. And even though they often rubbed each other the wrong way, each needed the other to exist.

David's long-term planning had given him the opportunity, the rock foundation on which to indulge himself now. And Emma's early life of indulgence, her sensual appetite, which fed on both flesh and ideas, gave not one thought to the future and yet she had found David.

David was going to be late for a meeting if he stood by the bed any longer but he found her form irresistible. The strong tea darkness of the room was broken by little sunbeams highlighting folds in the white bed clothes. The thick white sheet was like a second skin. Emma was lying on her stomach, one leg stretching for the corner of the bed and the other, knee slightly raised, reaching out to the other side, causing her lovely butt to be elevated provocatively. Even in her sleep, thought David.

And not for the first time he considered retiring. He had all that a man could desire. He had the funds to keep it. He and Emma could join Paul on one of his adventures, or head out on their own adventure. How often had he heard of people his age pulling the plug on their careers and moving to a coastal town and living a simple life? He'd never known any of these people personally, but they did exist. Surely.

He stood looking at his wife, he knew for certain what he would do in the first hour of retirement but couldn't see further than that. In fact, his thoughts of retirement always ended in this way. Why? Why would one retire? He loved what he did. He loved excelling. Why leave that? The form in front of him was one reason, no doubt, but then, didn't he make much of her already?

We can imagine Emma's horror on hearing such thoughts. Twenty-four-hour David would drive her mad. But, thankfully, David had never expressed them to her. In his mind retiring early was like retiring hurt, was like capitulating. He expressed it to himself and dwelt on it in secret. To express these thoughts to Emma would be to admit to a doubt he had in his abilities.

David stood at the end of the bed, contemplating what most men might have contemplated if faced with Emma's sleeping form, spread thus, under a clinging sheet. In this one thought he was entirely honest.

That was partly why Emma took such delight in the sexual. To look into someone's eyes and behold the untainted truth, to feel the truth – when else can someone be so sure? Any dope can tell if someone is abusing themselves and the truth of desire. It's in every movement they make. That was one reason Emma found little pleasure in fucking anyone paid to do so. She could find pleasure in it, but she doubted very much *their* pleasure. It was a great obscenity to her, a defilement of sexual truth, but then, Emma was quite capable of enjoying certain defilements.

David finished his coffee and placed the empty mug on the bedside table. He was very much tempted to wake his wife. He stood by her, leant his face towards hers and could sense how deeply she slept. Still the temptation lingered. He still thought her the most beautiful woman he'd seen. And even now, how powerfully she attracted him! Her loose dark hair, a representation of madness, covering part of her face, her shoulders and the pillow. It seemed now to beckon him, to have a life of its own.

Wake! he thought. Wake now!

He wanted to kiss her but knew from experience that this would wake her. He dreaded waking her and incurring her wrath, and this dread was greater than his need.

He was about to lift the sheet from her, just a little, to see her naked body, to smell her, but he heard the shrill ring of his mobile coming from the pocket of his suit jacket which he'd left in the kitchen.

He turned quickly and left his wife and the many signs on her alabaster body of the very physical activity her body had endured hours before (and the foreign scents still remaining after the hasty shower an exhausted Emma had had before collapsing into bed at dawn).

Hours later Emma stood naked before the full-length mirror in the corner of her room. The sun now hung high above the house already into its descent westward. Having opened the shutters and the doors she examined in broad daylight the marks left upon her by an enthusiastic Jason. She wasn't happy with what she found.

When she woke she'd been so very aroused. She'd been shaking with desire. She'd lain in bed luxuriating in an orgy of sensual memory and had made herself come four times in succession before she felt the shadow of calm.

The urgency she was experiencing subsided somewhat. But did not go away. She felt thoroughly sexual. Every movement reminded her of the fact. No amount of masturbation could cure her. Her toes rubbed themselves against the corner of the mattress and she felt if she kept doing so she could bring herself to orgasm.

She hadn't fully shaken sleep. Anything was possible. Her head was full of impressions – warmth, the texture of Egyptian cotton against her and beneath her, her wetness, summer sounds, Jason and all that made him desirable, David's scent, the artificial darkness of her room and a million others. Impressions wafted unimpeded through her mind.

This went on for a good twenty minutes before it occurred to her that some of the urgency she was feeling was, in fact, a very real need to pee.

Catching herself in the bathroom mirror as she passed by prompted her, after her pee, to open the shutters and make a thorough inspection of herself before the full-length mirror.

It was then that she realised she'd been naked and uncovered when she woke. Thank goodness for the shutters, but even so, David would have seen the bruises. Surely! Alabaster skin was all well and good but when it came to having passionate sex no skin could be more telling.

She turned and twisted and bent and lifted and could almost read the marks like a script. Not that it was truly, entirely Jason's fault. He was completely inexperienced and male, so his ability for prophesy was disabled by his innate disregard of thought. No, she was being harsh. But Jesus! How could she explain or hide this? This? These.

Failing her own high standards she fell for the circumstantial evidence and convinced herself that David had seen the marks. She pondered whether to wait and see if he revealed his knowledge to her in his eyes, or to come clean, ring him up and brazenly tell him what she did. In her dream world she would have that relationship with her husband

and in the beginning when everything she did was seen by him as exciting she might have got away with it. But now, David was closing the door to that kind of life. And he expected her to do the same. He thought Emma would grow out of her flirty ways.

Emma sat on her bed and considered her options. She found the whole situation distasteful. David's narrow vision was closing in on her. It was galling to her. She had married someone with whom she couldn't share the excitement of fucking an eighteen-year-old!

She'd come so far in life, had fought so many prejudices and narrow world views only to have married someone who appreciated, but could not accept, her ambition. To think that David loved her for who she was, and at the same time who she was was the one thing he wanted her to change. He didn't see it that way. But surely if she excited him like no other, as he claimed time and time again, he knew the reason why! It wasn't her beauty – there are so many beautiful women. It was her unbridled sensuality, her unrepentant, unfaithful, illicit, unimpeded, dirty, greedy, pleasure-seeking, pleasure-giving, hedonistic, altruistic, experienced, self-assured, voracious, loving, lusting self!

There were people she could share this knowl-edge with. She knew it, but they were few and not so emotionally involved. David was in the thick of it. His pride was involved. His male vision of right and wrong. His mother's vision too. Hell, the whole world was on his side. Narrow bunch that they were.

How tired she felt then.

The whole world vs Emma.

Could she continue?

Of course she could, but now she would have to lie far more than she liked to. She would have to live beside a man whose knowledge of her would always be patchy at best. But then, when hadn't she felt somewhat manipulative in her relations with people? Puppet-master Emma.

She should have told David about Jason the day he jumped over the fence. Why hadn't she? She knew damn well why she hadn't. It was the same then as it was now.

The day had started off so well.

TWENTY-TWO

Jason couldn't remember the start of his day. He was in the middle of third period before he knew himself. But even then he was more in touch with his reminiscences of the previous night than the classroom in which he sat. When he did take note of his immediate surroundings they were distasteful. Somehow the desk seemed smaller. The chattering of his fellow students seemed more adolescent than he had previously noted. He much preferred to dwell on last night. So much food for thought there, so little in this vast institute of learning.

By the end of lunch he had been insolent to two teachers and one form master (who promptly awarded him a detention notice), he had insulted his best friend, had found himself unable to eat, although he was ravenous, and had provoked a scuffle with the school bully in a stairwell and won outright. He then sat through the last two periods watching the clock and left school before the teacher had dismissed them, ignoring the detention notice and boarding the early bus home.

On the bus he pulled off his tie, untucked his shirt and stared aggressively at the other children. No one sat next to him. But their noises and antics were soon irritating enough for him to start thinking of getting off and walking. He'd finally had enough at Cremorne and pressed the button.

Once off the bus he stood dazed in the bright afternoon light. He was feeling so unusually aware. Tired and hungry and almost distraught after the day at school, he stood beside busy Military Road and watched the four lanes of speeding traffic fly past him with a strange new clarity.

He began walking home.

He was more tired than he knew, but his natural and habitual buoyancy kept him moving, kept him from realising how taxing each step was to him. He was experiencing that alert state of mind we sometimes encounter when all our major faculties are shut down in order to save on energy. Jason felt more alive than ever and this was because his whole being was experiencing something like tunnel vision. He crossed streets safely, negotiated uneven pavement, dodged dog poo and tree roots. But his focus was on women.

He had never noticed just how many attractive women there were on any given street.

He was noticing women twice Emma's age, young girls, and even noting the faces of women flashing past in their cars.

It was obvious to Jason that having attracted Emma and having done what they had together it followed he could attract all women and behave with them in a like manner.

He hovered at the intersection of Spofforth Street and Military Road just to watch for a moment. Three changes of lights and at least fifty wonderful sightings later he moved on.

He was bold in his appreciation too. Catching many a woman's eye and holding it till they looked away in confusion. Such confidence in a young man, standing erect in his dishevelled school uniform . . .

Emma's appreciation of Jason was not a quirk, he was an attractive specimen made more so by this newly acquired self-possession.

Time would not erase, nothing ever would erase, the final three hours he and Emma fell to after all that foolish play. Nor the lessons learnt therein. If Jason was bold he had every right to be.

He moved on.

Near the big furniture shop at the end of Glover Street he walked behind a woman pushing a stroller. He might easily have passed her but he attuned his step to hers. The sway of her hips was intoxicating, in the true sense of the word. She held the young man captivated for a hundred metres till their paths diverged and she had no idea. Nor would she know just what kind of young man she had metres behind her, for she had spent the whole time chattering away nonsensically with her two-year-old daughter.

Jason was no longer able to appraise what he saw according to the fashions of the day. He was attuned to a woman's erotic potential, not the size of her hips or breasts. Unthinkingly he was picking out what it was that attracted their men to them, his personal tastes had not truly formed. Some were beautiful but some were not. He was aroused nonetheless and it was something in particular in each instance. The woman pushing the stroller had wide hips and her buttocks wobbled grossly with each step, but it was the rhythm of her walk and the timing of the sway which held him there. Jason saw her naked and felt her weight rising and falling on him.

But then he turned down Belmont Road and she continued along Military Road.

In his rush that morning Jason had forgotten to charge his phone and so was forced to judge the time by the afternoon light. The walk was taking far longer than he had anticipated. He was bored. All the women had vanished. He was quite alone in his seemingly endless tramp along the dull pavement. The school bag on his shoulder was irksome. He considered leaving it somewhere. He had no need of it now. He wasn't going back to school. He was done with being told what to do.

Why had he alighted from the bus? He'd have been home by now. He'd have been with Emma. If he could get to a payphone he could call her and she could pick him up. They would just drive off together. Jason's parents owned a holiday house on the Central Coast. They could drive up there and hide out.

Thoughts like these made the walk endurable. So lost was he in his desperate conjugations that the halfway mark was passed unnoticed. As he drew nearer the end of the road his thoughts shifted from Emma to the other female in his life, young Jess. For it was her habit, after school, to sit with her friends on the far side of Border Oval, smoking and talking till dusk. Jason had occasionally joined her there. And now he was nearby and he had, only the night before, promised to meet her there that very afternoon. He could hardly believe that only one day had passed since giving his promise to her. Less than a full day. Jess could not imagine the changes he'd undergone since they last spoke. Nor could he.

He was annoyed with himself when he finally reached the park for he knew by the way the soft orange light was colouring the tops of the trees on the far side of the oval that Jess would be gone. He stood for a moment. He felt so very tired then. The park was near deserted as he began to walk through it. There was a father pushing a hard-core all-terrain stroller vigorously up the gentle slope towards the main road and a guy Jason had seen before, about his age, who was jogging round and round the oval. He leant against the white picket fence which circled the oval and let out an audible sigh. He had no option now but to go home. He found the energy to jump the fence and began the walk across the field.

He had missed Jess, had probably missed Emma and most likely, the way he was feeling and the pace he was now walking, would reach home after his parents.

So what did it matter?

Halfway across the field he looked up at the sky and saw a lovely pale blue, then down at the dull green grass and knew what to do. Moments later he was lying on his back staring up at the sky. Memories of the previous night's antics flooded in on him. The fragrant close-cropped grass differed from Emma's luxurious thick, long lawn but then grass was grass to the unobservant and he was lying on grass was he not?

He closed his eyes and drifted off to sleep.

TWENTY-THREE

Across the other side of the oval, in the secluded sanctuary between the line of trees that followed the curve of the oval and the picket fence itself, Jess sat with her friends. She had been on the lookout for Jason and had encouraged the group to stay seated by making no move to leave.

The girls had their own reasons for wanting to leave. It was becoming steadily cooler and as each of them attended school near naked they were seated on the cool ground shivering and holding their young male friends chastely but needfully. Each had at least one parent who would complain of their being late home, again. There was home-work to be done, TV to be watched, the web to be surfed and long repetitive phone conversations to be had with the very people they were talking languidly with now.

Jess had reason to stay, but none of the others did. Even though she was the unacknowledged leader of this lacklustre group of friends, she could not hold them indefinitely.

She was thankful then when she spied her young boyfriend jumping the far fence. She watched in disbelief as he lay down on his back in the middle of the oval. She rose unsteadily and her friends all jumped up too. In a flash they were off in all directions and Jess was alone. She climbed up and over the fence, no mean trick for a modest girl in an immodest short denim skirt.

Jess was trembling by the time she reached his prone form. The previous night's conversa-tion on the phone had awakened an expectation of some further sign, or verbalisation of his feel-ings towards her. His voice on the phone had been highly charged and each statement seemed to carry undercurrents of sensual meaning. Jess was highly alert to such sensuality. She was starved of physical attention.

Jason was asleep. She saw that immediately. She stood over him and shook her head. He looked pale, worn out and more dishevelled than she'd ever seen him. How adorable! She wanted to lie down and snuggle into his side. Should she nudge him with her foot?

'Hey!' she said loudly, and then, 'Boofhead!'

Nothing. The boy was dead to the world. Jess found this strange. Especially as he had come to meet her as he'd promised. Why fall asleep in the middle of the oval? In a moment of unusual daring she placed a foot at either side of his chest, straddling him, then sat down on his stomach like a naughty little kid.

The rash act did the trick, he woke but what happened next wasn't to plan. He pulled her down to him and kissed her, holding her closed lips against his till she gave in and opened them and accepted his kiss and warmed to it.

Jason barely knew who he was kissing. Emma was everywhere, filling all of his senses. She had been with him in sleep and had woken with him. Jess was there too. Her kiss differed greatly, her scent was raw, her tongue timid and her presence on his body near weightless. She was at least a foot shorter than Emma and of such a slight build that Jason soon realised that he had made a very fortunate mistake.

Jess was now kissing Jason with the full force of all her suddenly released emotions. She assumed that he had lain a trap for her and she had fallen in. Thank God! she thought. He held her so tightly and his kisses were by no means those of an inexperienced boy. In fact his right hand was gripping her bottom and the other was lost in her hair, holding her mouth to his. The other fact was that he was evidently hard. This she felt unmistakably, for it was pressing against her with evil intent.

Jason was unwilling to let her from his grip. This accidental turn was further proof of his extraordinary way with women. Emma had been good enough to show him the way and now he could take whom he wanted, when he wanted. And to think how nervous he'd been with Jess in the past. All he had had to do was take her. He was astonished by this revelation. His mind raced ahead to see who else he might have. But he was distracted on his rapid advance by Jess as she pressed herself heavily down against the hard bulge in his school pants. Her kiss became more forceful and Jason was taken in by her and his mind shut down and his body took over. This girl had much to express.

Though she was technically a virgin Jess was not inexperienced. She had always had boyfriends of a kind and each had pushed her in their own way for more than her peers would allow. She had to be very conscious of the group and those others in her year. Most were happy to make out and then go home to masturbate. She'd only once given a boy help in that and it had been very exciting. The stuff shot out all over her. She had never been as worked up since then. If there was one recurrent fantasy in her young life, that was it.

But now she felt Jason's passion rise a level and knew he was determined to take her with him.

He rolled her onto her back, lying on his side next to her, not breaking their kiss, and ran his hand up and down her inner thigh, brushing the cotton of her exposed knickers on each downward turn.

His kisses changed too. He slowed her frenetic pace and gently persuaded her to accept a different kind of kiss, one that lingered, one that took note of the sensitivity of their lips and thrilled her like never before. Her whole body tingled. His hand on her thigh was never more welcome. He kissed her like this for ever so long and soon dear Jess was so far gone she accepted without demure the full palm of his hand slipping between her legs, covering her mound.

How warm his hand felt and how natural that it should feel this way and be where it was. But his kisses! Her whole body seemed to be connected to his lips.

How hot she felt! She couldn't restrain a soft tender moan as his fingers pressed softly against her.

He was a bad boy. He knew what he was doing. And how happy she was that he should.

An hour later Jason was strolling towards Mosman Junction. He was so hungry and his mood had changed again and was back squarely at open rebellion.

He lifted his hand to his nose and breathed in the scent left by his new girlfriend. Each finger in turn. The smile on his face was devilish. Nothing would stop him now. He'd have a chicken and gravy roll and hot chips. Fuck dinner, he thought. What violence raged through his body! What power!

The body and mind of the boy was so exhausted but his ego was tireless and eager to fly.

When he reached the main road he once again

began his new trick of devouring and challenging each and every female he saw.

Each of his looks was received in a differing light, but incredulous might have been the general tone once he'd passed on. He certainly had a naked, open and utterly sexual look to give. And the incredulity of the women came from the realisation that there was an assumption of their acquiescence in the look. Which, if some of the women were honest with themselves, there was! The bold assumption was not a put-on, it was there, part of his makeup, unmistakable, palpable and thoroughly disarming in its honesty.

Caught unawares by a bold look from an unexpected quarter, some of the women he passed responded with more spirit than even they knew they had left in them. The young man was too enamoured of this new power to make an inventory of his successes or failures as he strolled and followed up none of the returns of serve. His was an assumption of success, and his was the enviable position, that he could pick or choose.

The shops were caught in that dusk of retail when late customers hope for extended opening hours and the retailers themselves, aware of the financial benefits of patience, have none to give. Gruff, ill-tempered men in suits manage by monosyllabic instruction to buy the wrong potatoes, a packet of unnecessary batteries, soap, and forget whatever it was their wives specifically asked them to pick up. All the while they make a nuisance of themselves by standing in the wrong place, blocking others, while surreptitiously looking at the photo of the latest starlet on the cover of a trashy magazine or, more specifically, looking at her fake breasts. Then they may try to pay with a cheque for naturally they have no cash, till it is made clear that, yes, they may use their credit card.

Jason strolled through all this clamour and haste with the simple intention of buying his takeaway. He knew well that dinner was waiting for him on his return home, but home was the last place he wanted to head.

Home for now was a reminder, like school was a reminder, that he was still a boy. These women on the street, the smells on his fingers, the memories of the previous night and the ache in his body were dearer to him because they said – you are a man. The more he thought of home, the stronger the aversion. The explanations he would have to make for his lateness seemed too heavy an obligation. He banished from his mind his mother's scrutiny, his father's silence and their combined love for him.

Up ahead of him, and moving in the same direction as he, a female figure more alluring than any other thus far made her way through the foot traffic. Tall, slender and holding herself straight, she moved quickly and determinedly without losing any of her self-possession. From the back Jason was enthralled, he quickened his pace.

The woman was wearing backless sandals, clip-clopping along, a loose black skirt that fell below the knee but hung low on her hips, revealing her back dimples, and a tight black singlet top which needed to be pulled down after every step if she wanted to remain decent.

The woman up ahead seemed not to pay attention to such things. Jason watched her hips swish back and forth with each step, then, as he drew nearer he felt a fool, for the stranger turned into Emma. Now having her so identified, he was astonished that he could have failed to recognise her. Her hair was up. That was it. No. He'd seen her often enough with it up. She was wearing black, that was the difference.

He followed her into the mini-market.

TWENTY-FOUR

Emma's day had been one of idleness, of recovery and of frustrated desire. With every step she took, with every movement of her arms, with every turn of her head she returned to the night before. Her body ached in a good way. She could do nothing unconsciously. Every muscle reminded her of what she'd done. Jason's hands were still on her. He was still in her. Everything aroused her. Standing at the back door, a fresh breeze blowing her hair, she acknowledged that her night with Jason had been no minor indiscretion. Fucking the neighbours' son was an act of defiance. This was not the act of a bored housewife. This was a return to the Emma she had always been. The Emma she knew she should be.

She called Paul. He said he would be right over.

As Emma showered and dressed she willed Paul to come quickly. She feared she might change her mind.

There was a knock at the door. Emma dashed downstairs. There he stood, in the flesh, as handsome as ever. He said nothing and stepped into the house and closed the door.

He looked her in the eye as though searching for something. His unbroken gaze excited her.

He knew! He knew! The slightest movement of his eyebrow said as clearly as speech, *You've been wicked.*

She could hide nothing from Paul. He reached around her and grabbed her backside and drew her to him. He knew what she wanted. He knew how she wanted it. He had been here many times before. He accepted his role.

He spun her around and bit down on her neck. She pushed her butt into his crotch. He thrust his hand down the front of her jeans. His fingers found her waiting for him. She ground against him.

Emma was pushed against the wall. He

unbuttoned her and drew down her jeans. She reached around and fumbled with his fly. Impatient, he moved her hand aside and released himself. Tearing down her G-string with one hand he gripped himself with the other.

'You're a very bad girl, Emma,' he said as he entered her.

After Paul had gone Emma had a very hot bath. She lay back and turned on the bubbles. Paul's visit had settled it. She was never going back. She loved David, but she was never going to be entirely his. She would have to lie to him. She would have to deceive. To do otherwise was to deceive herself. In an hour or so Jason would walk through the back door and she would lead him to her marriage bed. She would. Jason adored her. He had come so far in such a short time. The way he had taken her again and again in the early hours of the morning . . . this was not the boy who had jumped over the fence. Emma knew she was responsible for this change. And now he would come to her and show yet another side to himself. Even with all her experience with men she realised she had no idea what this might be.

It was now almost five and Jason had not arrived. Emma lounged on the day bed on her balcony. She wrapped a blanket around her and tried his mobile again. It went straight to messages. She cancelled the call.

It hadn't crossed her mind that he wouldn't turn up. She was shocked. She couldn't help but feel hurt. She tried to remember what he had said when he left her at dawn. She had been exhausted, she remembered. She couldn't recall what he had said. She did recall that he had been willing to go on. She had said no. The temperature had plummeted and they had been wrapped in the blankets. At her no, he had stood in naked perfection. He had raised his arms in the blue light of dawn, stretching out towards the sky, and would have roared like some beast had it been possible. He looked like a conqueror. Even then, after hours of fucking, his cock seemed unwilling to expire. It hung thick, caught between two worlds.

He had then reached down, taking her hand, and pulled her upright. It was he who had led her to the back door and had sent her off to bed. She had locked the back door and watched him as he had picked up his clothes and walked, still nude, towards the side passage.

He hadn't said he would come to her the following afternoon, she now remembered. But she had assumed he would.

As daylight waned and her patience ended she decided to raise herself from disappointment. She had nothing in the house for dinner. She would head up to the shops.

After parking illegally in the evening rush hour she'd walked briskly to the supermarket and on arrival had realised she had no desire to cook or to shop or to even breathe.

Jason had followed Emma in, making sure she did not see him. The mini-market was deep and narrow with only three poorly lit aisles stacked to the high ceiling with boxes atop of the shelves. Lines of disgruntled shoppers stood waiting their turn at the checkout, juggling necessary and unnecessary items in their arms.

Jason watched from just inside the door as Emma negotiated her way through them, lifting a basket from the stack as she went. He passed by the checkout counters and hovered at the end of the first aisle to see how far Emma intended to go.

He now knew what he wanted to do to her. The skirt she was wearing had been his inspiration.

Jason followed her as she made her way to the very back of the mini-market. Rounding the corner he found Emma at the freezers holding one of the doors open. Her back was to him. He could hear people around the corner. Would Mrs Emma Benson approve of any public display of affection? There was no time to reason it out.

Emma was having trouble deciding what she wanted. One of the checkout girls had looked a lot like Jason's Jess. And this had started Emma thinking about her. Jason would go to Jess with all that she had taught him. It was unavoidable. It was even possible he did so this afternoon. This thought was painful to Emma. It tasted bitter. Would he do such a thing? And then she remembered how he had taken her that morning. He had exulted in his newborn powers.

These thoughts were interrupted. While looking for frozen peas she felt her skirt rise and then felt a warm hand smooth swiftly along her thigh before coming to rest between her slightly parted legs.

She spun around quickly, ready to hit out at her attacker but found Jason in his school uniform staring at her with a frightened expression.

'Fucking hell, Jason!' She started hitting his chest with open palms. 'What the fuck!'

Jason was devastated by this reaction. He took a few steps backwards. A man came around the corner and walked between them. He eyed both with interest before moving on.

'Have you gone mad?' whispered Emma. 'What the hell are you thinking? You scared the crap out of me.'

'I couldn't help it,' said Jason truthfully.

'Oh, Jesus.' Emma picked up the basket she had placed on the floor. 'I can't be seen with you. This is insane. You have to go. I'll see you tomorrow.'

'I'm not going.' He stepped closer to her, his confidence returning. What right had she to dismiss him?

'Go, before somebody sees us.'

'I'll go if you do something for me.'

A middle-aged woman rounded the corner. Emma knew her face. She worked in the bank. She opened the freezer door beside Emma. They both waited until she had moved on.

'Why didn't you come this afternoon?'

'Got detention for swearing at a teacher,' he lied. 'Let me touch you.'

'No!' she said.

'Yes,' he said, coming even closer. He took hold of the hem of her skirt. Anyone rounding the corner now would have no doubt what was going on.

'Not here.'

'Yes, here.'

'No, Jason.'

'Then give me something. Give me your undies. Take them off for me.'

Emma couldn't think. He was exciting her. She pulled the skirt from his fingers.

'I'm not going until you give them to me.'

'Will you come to me tonight?'

'I could take you here and now. It's all I want to do from now on.'

Emma hesitated. She wanted to give them to him. She was trembling. She could hear voices. A group of teenage girls rounded the corner. They were chatting loudly. Behind their backs, as they passed by, Emma quickly lifted her skirt, pulled down her undies, stepped out of them and scrunched the tiny G-string in her hand.

Jason had watched her thinking only of her naked pussy. He was rock hard when she handed him the warm bundle. He raised it to his nose and then pushed it into his pocket.

'Now go.'

With that, he rushed off.

Emma waited a minute or two then followed. She had been so aroused by her young lover's confidence. He was bold. Imperious. He had shown her he was willing to break the rules. She had been so frightened when she felt his hand touching her. All of her adolescent fears had returned. But as soon as she saw his face she had marvelled at his audacity. He hadn't pressed home his advantage. He had won her G-string. He might have taken more.

Having taken four or five steps down the middle aisle, Emma heard Jason's mother, Anne. Horrified, she stopped and listened.

'We agreed to the plan. You said you would keep to it.'

'I arranged to meet Jess before I agreed to your plan. I just forgot.'

'Jason, it's not good enough. We've worked too hard.'

'I'll do twice as much tomorrow.'

'You've lost a full day. You can't do this to us now. You'll have plenty of time to waste after your exams.'

'My time with Jess was not a waste. I need to

have a life, too. If you keep pressuring me I'll just give up.'

Emma had heard enough.

∞

Jason was stuck talking to his mother while she shopped. They had not come across Emma as they did so. Jason was really hoping Emma had left and had not overheard him tell his mother he had been with Jess. He knew it wouldn't sound good. What a fool he had been to get off the bus. If he had gone straight home he would have spent the afternoon fucking Emma. He felt exhausted just thinking about the consequence of that one stupid act. Now he was carrying his mother's shopping basket.

He diverted his anger at himself towards his mother. She was always interfering. He was over being the good son. He was over it. He'd been good, he'd been predictable, and where had that got him?

Only five minutes ago when his hand had lifted Emma's skirt he had been shaking. When his hand touched her between her legs the blood pounded in his temples. Her sudden and violent reaction had frightened and excited him in an extraordinary way. Her blows against his chest accentuated his already heightened sense of the indecency of his actions.

Everything had changed but his mother remained the same. He had done with being good. Bad was working very well for him.

When Emma overheard that Jason had spent the afternoon with Jess she was not surprised. But she was hurt. Her pride was a little shaken too. She exited the mini-market right away. She could not bear to look at him. When she got to her car she found she had been given a parking ticket. She ripped the slip of paper from under the wind-screen wiper and got into her car, slamming the door as she did so.

Three minutes later she was sitting in her car outside her house. David's BMW was in the drive-way. She couldn't face him. She didn't have the strength to hide her feelings. She didn't want to lie. If she walked in now, everything would have to be false. He deserved better than that. She started the car again and drove off.

Trouble was, she had no idea where she was going.

TWENTY-FIVE

Jason had been on the lookout for David. His attempts to contact Emma had come to nothing. She had disappeared. Days and days had gone by without a word. He was left with no other choice. If he wanted to know where she was he would have to approach her husband. Trouble was, he was afraid David might not want to have anything to do with him.

He was afraid David knew what he and Emma had been doing together.

He was afraid David would snap his neck.

Emma's sudden disappearance the day after the

night they spent together in the backyard had but one probable cause: David had thrown her out. The improbable cause was that he had discovered what had happened and had beaten her to death with his bare hands.

For three days Jason was obsessed with the idea that David would come for him. That he would be beaten, or yelled at, or exposed before his parents. When the phone rang he was convinced it was David. He would hover nearby holding his breath until he was sure he was safe. When there was a knock at the door, he would take off down the hall and out the back so that he wouldn't have to answer it. He was a bundle of nerves. In the morning he dreaded hearing his father call out a hello to his neighbour. Leaving for work, the two men would occasionally speak briefly across the fence. He imagined them having a quick man-to-man chat.

'Your son fucked my wife,' David would say.

'It's only fair that you fuck mine,' his father would answer.

'I think I'd prefer to snap his neck.'

'She may not look like much but she knows what she's doing.'

'If it's all the same to you . . .'

'By all means, snap away. He has transgressed and he must be punished.'

But as the days passed and nothing happened Jason relaxed and reconsidered. If David knew Jason had been fucking his wife surely he'd have something to say about it? David had made no attempt to speak with him. Jason's neck had not been snapped. Nothing had happened at all. David seemed to be living much as he always had, leaving for work early and arriving home late.

Jason wanted to know where Emma was. He wanted to be with her. He wanted her. He could barely breathe when he thought of what they had done together. To find Emma he must ask someone where she had gone. He could ask his parents, but he didn't dare show an interest in her. He could break into her house to look for clues as to her whereabouts, as he knew where they kept the spare key, but when he attempted to do so he panicked at the first sound and scarpered. Or he could walk straight up to David and ask him where Emma was.

'I'd like to fuck your wife again; do you have any idea where she might be?'

Three nights running he was on his parents' verandah when David arrived home. He watched him park his car in the driveway and make his way up the path and the stairs to the front door. Jason might have called out to him from that safe distance but instead, each time, he had stepped out of view.

This state of affairs could not go on forever. Jason cursed himself for being a coward. He must act. And now.

Before he was ready Jason found himself standing by Emma and David's front gate. The sun had set. Light was fading. David had been home for half an hour or so. Jason pushed it open and forced himself up the stairs. He stood on the verandah. He felt unwell. He was actually trembling. He plunged his hand into his pocket where he found Emma's G-string. He gripped it for luck and lifted the knocker with his free hand and let it drop. The great hunk of iron created an impressive noise. He could hear it reverberate through the house.

But then nothing happened.

He was going to lift it again but thought better of it and, taking his chance, he began to skip down the steps. He was halfway to the gate when he heard, 'Who is it?'

The call came not from the front door, but from above.

Jason swung around and glanced up.

David was leaning over the top balcony railing with a cigarette in one hand and a beer in the other.

He flicked the cigarette off into the night.

'I'll come down.'

Jason climbed the steps reluctantly, his feet heavy. David took his time. To Jason it felt a lifetime. He hovered on the top step, well out of reach, just in case things turned bad.

When David opened the door, Jason flinched and stumbled backwards. He gathered himself, but only after he had reached down, taking hold of the lip of the top step. He stood up and found David watching him with a grin.

'Evening,' said David. He took a sip of his beer.

'Emma said she was . . . book,' said Jason, tangled by his own tongue. He hadn't thought what he was going to say. What possible reason could he have for wanting to know where Emma was? He was an idiot.

'What?' asked David, with a chuckle.

'Is Emma home? She promised to lend me . . . She's been tutoring me,' he stammered, finding the truth eventually. She *had* been tutoring him.

'Nah, mate. She's gone away for a few days. Up the coast with a girlfriend.'

'She didn't say anything . . . That's okay.'

'She didn't say anything to me either, mate. Emma's full of surprises. What book do you need?'

'A book for school. She said she would lend it to me.'

'I can't help you with that stuff. Do you want to go and have a look for it? I can show you where she keeps them.'

'Thanks, I'll find them.'

David stood aside and let the boy through.

Jason made a beeline for the bookcase in the upstairs passageway and knelt on the floor. He was shaking. He had no idea what he was doing.

'Have you and Emma been working together?' asked David from the top of the stairs.

Jason jumped. He thought David had stayed downstairs.

'English. She's been helping me.'

'She's left us both in a lurch then,' said David. 'Never trust the pretty ones.'

Jason had nothing to say to this.

'It's all right if you think she's pretty, mate. She's fucking gorgeous. If I were your age I'd kill for a tutor who looked like her.'

Jason turned back to the bookcase and grabbed an orange-covered paperback, then stood up.

'What is it?' asked David, coming closer.

Jason had no idea what he had picked so he handed it to David.

'That saucy minx,' he said. 'Did she ask you to read this?'

David held it up. It was *Lady Chatterley's Lover*.

'It's for school.'

'Do you know what it's about?'

'Nup,' said Jason, which was true.

'I've never read it. But it's meant to be filthy.'

The phone rang.

David went off to answer it.

Jason hovered for a moment in the passage-way. He just could not work out David. Was he trying to warn him off? Was he trying to tease out some information? Or was what he said true? Had Emma just taken off? Were they both in the same boat?

Jason was sure of only one thing. He wasn't going to wait around to find out. He made his way quickly and quietly out of the house. If Emma was done with him, he was done with Emma.

TWENTY-SIX

At her friend Sally's beach house, Emma stood at the open balcony door, a glass of white wine in her hand, listening to the waves, with their occasional distant booms. Her bare feet were slightly sandy from a day spent on the beach. The floorboards were smooth and cool beneath them. Her skin was dry and salty. She still wore her bikini beneath her sundress. Around her shoulders she had draped one of the throws Sally's mother had bought for the couches.

With nightfall came a sudden drop in temperature. She sipped the cool wine, enjoying its clean taste. The night beyond the balcony was darker than Emma had remembered it ever having been. The houses to the left and the right of them were all vacant. The holiday season had yet to begin.

Looking out she could not see a thing. The ocean swallowed up everything. The pale grey floorboards of the balcony, and the reflections on the glass railing, seemed suspended in a void; not a star, nor lights from a passing ship, could she see.

Behind Emma, Sally was bustling about in the kitchen. She could hear the clatter of pots, the jingle of the opening and closing fridge door laden with wine bottles, and subdued mumbles as Sally spoke to her husband on the mobile that was tucked between her ear and shoulder. Food was being prepared, the earthy aroma of garlic wafted, the orange lampshades were ablaze, casting muted warm tones over the room.

After dinner the two women took their glasses and a bottle of wine and sat down to watch *To Catch a Thief*. On the lounge in the blue flickering light Emma snuggled up to Sally who welcomed the contact. They had no need to speak, having fallen seamlessly into the ways of their teens.

Sally stroked Emma's hair. Emma closed her eyes. The movie was short and ended all too soon.

When Sally turned off the TV only the pale beam above the stove gave any light. Turning, Emma could look out down the coast to the lights of the houses around the village and those up on the hill that rose steeply behind it. She wandered over to the stove and switched the light off.

Sally stretched out on the lounge. The darkness shifted gradually as their eyes welcomed the scant light of the moonless night outside. Emma could not remain still. She roamed the room, viewing the shrouded world from the windows.

'I love coming up here for a weekend by myself in winter,' said Sally. 'At night I lie like this, with all the lights off, and listen to the surf. There really is no one up here midwinter, Em. It's bliss. People quite forget me. And I forget them. Do you know what that's like?'

'I do,' replied Emma, 'but now I'm very glad you're here with me.'

'I didn't mean I wish I was alone, Em. I love how we've run away together. It's very romantic. Like *Thelma and Louise*, minus the guns and the tragic end.'

'Or Virginia Woolf and Vita Sackville-West.'

'I suppose,' said Sally, having no idea what they were like, 'but it's more like *Thelma and Louise*.

You got yourself into trouble and I whisked you away.'

'And, darling, I thank you for it.'

'Now to find Brad Pitt.'

They were silenced by the thought of that man.

Emma padded over to Sally.

'But don't you get scared up here alone? I would.'

'You scared? I doubt it. Anyway it's scarier in Mosman. The more people there are the greater the chance of a weirdo, don't you think? All those big houses, silent as the grave, but not empty. I prefer these empty beach houses to those. Who knows who's watching from suburban windows?'

Emma lay down beside Sally.

'But I have never felt scared in Mosman. Last night I couldn't sleep for worry.'

'Poor baby! Sleep in my bed tonight then. I didn't sleep well, as you know. I miss my husband's body. Yours is nicer than his, so I should sleep wonderfully.'

'Remember how we used to sleep together as girls? We were rather wicked young girls.'

'You've always been more wicked than me, Em. I feel I've just come along for the ride.'

'Do you regret it?'

'Sometimes. There are so many things I can't talk about to anyone else but you. Mark doesn't really know who I am. Or what I'm capable of . . .'

'I love our secrets, Sal. I love our past. I regret nothing.'

'We've always been so different, Em.'

'I know.'

They lay together for some time, each thinking her own thoughts, while listening to the surf. By the time they stirred, their eyes were so accustomed to the darkness they were able to lock the doors and make their way upstairs without the need of lights.

Sally lit a candle to shower by and Emma sat nearby on the closed lid of the loo observing her.

The golden light of the flickering candle and the white tiles made her tan seem darker still. Her wet skin shimmered as she turned this way and that.

Staring at Sally's lovely long legs as she washed them with shower gel, feeling the pleasure derived from the close proximity of such beauty, Emma's mind kept drifting back to her night with Jason.

What did it matter to her if he had gone straight to Jess with all that she had given him? Jess would never experience a night like the one she and Jason had shared. Just as Paul would never share the nights she had with David, nor David the nights she had shared with Paul. She knew it was silly to be jealous of anybody. Her feelings had become entwined. She had tripped. She could untie them. She knew she had hurt David by leaving, but then her life was always going to be complicated. If she wanted to enjoy all that life offered she would have to be more careful.

She knew how fleeting beauty was. She was thirty-two. Her body was healthy and attractive. All too soon she would regret not having made more of this time when she could have confidence in herself, knowing herself beautiful, knowing a lover's words were truly meant, and their lust was attached to who she was now and not the person she had once been.

Jason's body was perfect and she had devoured it. The raw, undeniable effect beauty had on her was something splendid. She would not stop desiring it. Shallow? Maybe. But much in art was just as shallow. Beauty was intoxicating. Looking at Sally's back now affected her physically. The power of the sight blasted through her anxieties. The two halves of Sally's behind, the dimples in her lower back, were seductive. She was slim, no fat on her, lean and long.

Sally woke Emma out of her reverie.

'Shall I leave it on?' she asked. 'Will you shower?' she added, noticing Emma seemed dazed.

Emma nodded and stood to undress.

After showering Emma found Sally already in bed. She blew out the candle and in the sudden darkness stumbled towards the bed.

She already knew that she would find no rest, sleeping in a bed beside Sally.

She thought back to the conversation she'd had with Sally that evening, about the wicked things they'd got up to when they were younger.

She smiled as she drifted off to sleep.

Emma didn't believe in wicked pasts.

She believed wholeheartedly in wicked futures . . .

ACKNOWLEDGEMENTS

I wish to thank my agent and publisher for their much needed guidance. Thank you.

And thanks and love to my family, friends and above all my partner for supporting me throughout. Without your love and belief in me I would never have persisted. A big thank you and all my love.

If you enjoyed BEGINNINGS,
read on for a sneak peek of

The
SECRET
LIVES
OF EMMA
DISTRACTIONS

Coming October 2012 . . .

Emma moved quietly through the beach house in the dark. The house was silent. She went from room to room and her naked feet padded soundlessly on the polished floorboards. As she passed the kitchen she noticed the oven clock; it said it was half past four. She was looking for David. She had woken in bed having missed her husband's large, reassuring form. His side of the bed was empty and cold with the covers thrown back.

She darted through the beach house, her expectations rising at every new turn. She approached the downstairs bathroom and smiled to herself – why didn't I think of it? She was sure he was in there, but when she knocked softly and received no reply she suddenly panicked.

In the kitchen she called his name softly, reluctant to disturb Sally and Mark who were asleep upstairs. Again there was no reply. She stood in the kitchen worrying. He had never done this before. He was always so loud and he shook the bed so roughly when he went to the toilet in the middle of the night. This was different.

Emma rushed to the window overlooking the street. She wanted to know if his car was still parked outside. It was. She had had the idea he had gone. Gone, gone. Never before had she thought that David might just up and leave her. But there it was. David *might* just leave her. For good. For reasons he might never be able to explain. God, I'm so self-obsessed, she thought.

Still she had no idea where he was. Walking to the beach side of the house she could see the balcony. It was empty. Beyond, in the darkness, was the beach. She opened the glass sliding door slowly, making sure it didn't squeak.

'Emma,' said David from the darkness.

Emma jumped back, startled. 'What are you doing out here?'

'Couldn't sleep,' he said. He had been sitting on the railing with his back against the wall of the house, just out of view. He was wearing his dressing gown over his otherwise naked body. She immediately noticed that he was holding a lit cigarette.

'But you've quit!'

'Couldn't do it, Em,' he said, leading her across the balcony to the far railing, away from Sally and Mark's bedroom window, which was just above them. 'Not now. It's all too much at work.'

She stood motionless on the front verandah, still shaken by the shocking thought that he'd end their marriage. He was still here, but he wasn't himself. She had been so dishonest. Had he discovered something? Would he forgive her as she would forgive him?

'Have a smoke with me, Em,' he said, handing her a cigarette. She took it without considering what she was doing. She was in a bit of a daze.

Please tell me quickly, she was thinking, let me know now.

David waited for Emma to lift the cigarette to her mouth. He held the lit lighter in his cupped hands but she was miles away.

'Em? Are you awake?' he asked, with a smile.

'Sure,' she said. She didn't move, so he lifted her hand to her mouth. She smiled, laughing softly, and said, 'Sorry. No. I don't want it.'

David moved back to the railing. He looked out into the night. The dark ocean and the magnificent night sky.

'This isn't like you,' she said.

'What isn't?' he asked, turning back to her.

'Not sleeping, silly.' She wrapped her arms around his waist and hugged him.

'Maybe I had too much coffee,' he said. He drew heavily on the cigarette and exhaled dramatically.

'Tell me what's worrying you, baby.'

David walked up and down the verandah in the dark, smoking, answering some of Emma's whispered entreaties and telling her something of his troubles at work, but he was no less restless.

Emma was shivering. Behind her, away to the east, the dark night sky was being diluted, drop by drop, by pale, corrosive daylight. Time would not stand still for him. The night would end and he would have to face Emma in the clear light of day.

He had to tell her what he had only just whispered to himself. He stopped pacing and stood in front of her. He took her cold hands in his.

Emma's heart skipped a beat. He couldn't speak. He looked into her eyes.

'I want children,' he said.

Emma almost laughed. Her worst fears were unfounded. In her relief she failed to realise the importance of his words.

David viewed the situation differently. He wanted children. There were forces at work within him. The years had begun to pass by terrifyingly quickly and the issue of children of his own morphed from being a vague presumption into an urgent need. He had waited patiently for some sign from Emma. But none had come. He was now afraid that all he had built and all he had managed to achieve and Emma's love were all being risked by this roll of the dice.

Emma gathered herself after a moment.

'So do I,' she answered.

'Now?' he asked. 'I need to know.'

'Why do you need to know? What's gotten into you?'

'Something Dad said.'

Emma was at a loss. She didn't want children now. No. Not now or soon. Maybe not ever. And suddenly she felt the seriousness of the situation.

'You know he was twenty-four and Mum was

twenty-two when they had me,' continued David. 'He said the other day that you're never ready. But I disagree. I reckon I'm ready now. Look at what we've got. We can cope. We are in a better position to have children than most people ever are.'

All through the night David's thoughts had come back to one piece of knowledge. Emma was unlike any woman he had ever known. He had married her on the strength of that. And since the wedding he had had this view reinforced time and time again. No one had loved him like Emma had, no one had demonstrated their love as Emma had, but then conversely no one was as selfish as Emma. She was bigger than life, better than life and not of this life. Sometimes she seemed so far from him. He became a simple being and his needs became quaint beside hers. Career, wife, home, children. And yet, hadn't he married her?

'I'm ready, Emma. I really am,' he repeated. He still held her hands, still looked at her intently, but his words had no effect. She remained silent. She was looking into his eyes. 'I never would have dreamed that I would be the one saying all this. I never thought I'd be looking into my wife's eyes . . .'

Tears sprang from those eyes.

What could she tell him?

Fifty Shades
of Grey

E L James

FIFTY SHADES OF GREY

E. L. James

When Ana met Grey . . .

When literature student Anastasia Steele interviews successful entrepreneur Christian Grey, she finds him very attractive and deeply intimidating. Convinced that their meeting went badly, she tries to put him out of her mind – until he turns up at the store where she works part-time, and invites her out.

Unworldly and innocent, Ana is shocked to find she wants this man. And, when he warns her to keep her distance, it only makes her want him more.

But Grey is tormented by inner demons, and consumed by the need to control. As they embark on a passionate love affair, Ana discovers more about her own desires, as well as the dark secrets Grey keeps hidden away from public view . . .

Romantic, liberating and totally addictive, *Fifty Shades of Grey* is a novel that will obsess you, possess you, and stay with you for ever.

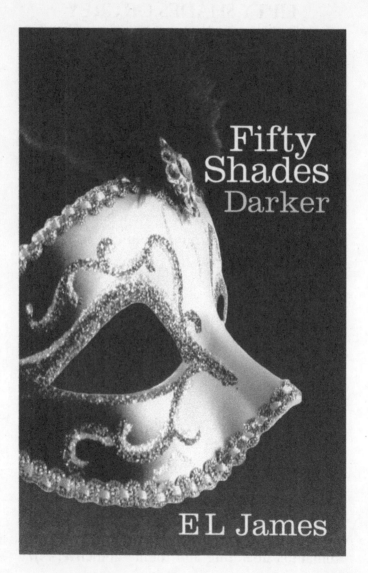

Fifty
Shades
Darker

E L James

FIFTY SHADES DARKER

E. L. James

What Ana and Grey did next . . .

Daunted by the dark secrets of the tormented young entrepreneur Christian Grey, Ana Steele has broken off their relationship to start a new career with a US publishing house.

But desire for Grey still dominates her every waking thought, and when he proposes a new arrangement, she cannot resist. Soon she is learning more about the harrowing past of her damaged, driven and demanding Fifty Shades than she ever thought possible.

But while Grey wrestles with his inner demons, Ana must make the most important decision of her life. And it's a decision she can only make on her own . . .

FIFTY SHADES FREED

Fifty
Shades
Freed

E L James

FIFTY SHADES FREED

E. L. James

Is a happy ending possible for Ana and Grey?

When Ana Steele first encountered the driven, damaged entrepreneur Christian Grey, it sparked a sensual affair that changed both their lives irrevocably.

Ana always knew that loving her Fifty Shades would not be easy, and being together poses challenges neither of them had anticipated. Ana must learn to share Grey's opulent lifestyle without sacrificing her own integrity or independence; and Grey must overcome his compulsion to control and lay to rest the horrors that still haunt him.

Now, finally together, they have love, passion, intimacy, wealth, and a world of infinite possibilities.

But just when it seems that they really do have it all, tragedy and fate combine to make Ana's worst nightmares come true . . .